M000098999

CULVER CREEK SERIES BOOK 4

BLOOD
ANSWER

ALISSA GROSSO

GLITTER
PIGEON
PRESS

UNTITLED

67,700 words.

UNTITLED

BLOOD ANSWER

by Alissa Grosso

1

IN THE ENTIRETY of his adult life, Sage Dorian had spent
no more than two weeks being unemployed, and it turned out
he wasn't especially good at it. He feared his lack of a job was
going to drive him insane.

Since being terminated from the Culver Creek police force
—unjustly, in his opinion—he had thrown himself into the
investigation of his sister's unsolved murder. He tried to force
himself to see his firing as a blessing, the forces of destiny
coming together to enable him to help Melodie receive the
justice she deserved. But the forces of destiny were not being
all that helpful.

Which was why Sage had decided to go for a walk to clear
his head. He had considered showering or at least putting on
some clean clothes before stepping out of the apartment that
was feeling more and more like a prison cell with each passing
day, then decided it was unlikely he would run into anyone he
knew on his stroll. That was because, other than the police and
a small handful of residents, he knew no one in Culver Creek.

Sometimes feeling like an outsider made him uncomfortable, but on this gray autumn day he welcomed the anonymity.

As he walked, he mentally reviewed the facts surrounding his sister's murder. What he knew was that for some reason Melodie had been murdered one night while driving home from work, and based on her behavior—she stepped out of her car late at night on a dark stretch of road and was facing her killer—it was someone she trusted.

Sage stopped short. A silver Toyota Prius rolled slowly down the road and, as Sage watched, turned left at the next intersection. Sage watched until it was out of sight. It was the same car. It had to be. He had seen it parked on his road, and on his brief excursions to the little grocery market in town, it always seemed to be there. What's more, he was sure he had seen it on his trips back to Pleasant Oaks as well. Someone was following him.

Sage took off at a jog down the sidewalk and hung a left at the next corner. He was on what passed for Culver Creek's main drag and thus in more danger of running into a familiar face, but he didn't care about that anymore. Because halfway down the block on the opposite side of the road, the silver Prius had found a parking spot. Sage noted the Sierra Club and Environmental Defense Fund stickers on the back bumper, which seemed almost too on point for someone driving a Prius. Then he dashed across the road, not bothering to look for oncoming cars, forcing some guy in a pickup truck to slam on his brakes before leaning angrily on his horn and shouting at Sage to watch where he was going. Sage paid him no mind.

Instead he banged on the driver's side window of the Prius. The driver was still behind the wheel, and he jumped. Sage motioned for the guy to roll down his window. The guy tried to wave Sage away from the car, but Sage refused to budge. He wanted answers. The guy made a back-off motion again, and this time Sage noticed the guy was trying to open his door. So Sage took a step backward into the road, earning him another toot from a passing motorist's horn. Had Culver Creek's struggling downtown ever seen so much traffic?

The bearded guy in a fleece jacket and hiking boots who stepped out of the Prius looked like he would have been more comfortable walking a trail at the state park. He didn't strike Sage as particularly menacing, and Sage certainly couldn't recall ever having seen him before. So why the hell was this guy following him around?

For a second, Sage thought he had made a mistake. Maybe this wasn't the same silver car he had spotted tailing him. He was working out an appropriate apology when the guy said, "TruthSeeker900?"

That caught Sage off guard. So much so that he took another staggering step backward. This time at least there was no oncoming car. He nodded his response to the mystery man and squinted at his bearded visage, trying to match the face up with some long-forgotten avatar, but the web sleuth crowd tended to be a paranoid bunch who hid their identities behind things like weapons or random images pulled from the internet as opposed to selfies and snapshots.

"Who are you?" Sage asked.

"Well, most likely you know me as PhillyFury."

PhillyFury. There was a name from his past. After his sister's murder and before he had ever donned a police officer's uniform, Sage had become addicted to online crime-solving forums. The web sleuth message boards, like anywhere on the internet, attracted a fairly odd mix of characters. The majority seemed to be troublemakers and time-wasters, but there were some who took the forum's aim to solve crimes seriously, and there was a select band of users for whom Sage had respect. The username PhillyFury belonged to that select group.

Seeing the face that matched the username was somewhat dizzying. The experience of meeting someone who he had only known online was one that he'd had a few times previously. It never ceased to be weird and disorienting when the real world and the online world collided.

A horn sounded, and Sage looked up to see a maroon sedan headed down the road.

"We should probably talk," PhillyFury said. "You want to grab a coffee?"

He waved in the direction of the sidewalk, and Sage saw they were just outside of Culver Creek's coffee shop.

2

IT TOOK Justin Turner a massive amount of effort to not jiggle his leg as he sat across from his caseworker. He shouldn't have been nervous delivering good news, but he could tell Ambrose was not pleased.

There were lots of little clues. For starters, there was the face he was making, like he was changing a disgusting dirty diaper or carrying a foul-smelling garbage bag out to the curb. Ambrose had the body language of someone trying to figure out how to best go about delivering a contrary opinion. And then there was the voice in his head that told him his caseworker thought he was a first-class headcase and wished he didn't always get stuck with all the weirdos.

"So we discussed looking for employment when we met last week," Ambrose said in a strained but professional voice.

"And I was able to get a job," Justin said. "It's not perfect, but I think it will work out well."

Not perfect was an understatement. Working at what basically amounted to a psychic sweatshop was far from his idea of a dream job, but it was work. Sometimes he wondered if things had turned out different, what sort of career he might have had. He thought he would be good at Ambrose's job. In fact, he was pretty sure he would be better at it than his caseworker was. But Virgil Chandler's record meant a job like that would never be a possibility for him. He was stuck with bottom-of-the-barrel jobs.

"Tell me more about this job," Ambrose said.

"It's a call center," Justin explained. "People phone in for free readings."

"Psychic stuff," Ambrose said.

"It's just tarot cards," he said. "It's not real."

"Because no fortune telling, psychic mumbo jumbo stuff is real, right?" Ambrose asked. He was using the sort of voice one used with toddlers.

Who does he think he is? Treating you like an idiot when you know way more than he does. Unbelievable! He ignored the outraged words that came into his head from another realm.

Ambrose took off his reading glasses, set them down on the desk, and massaged his eyes.

"Do you think it's such a good idea to work at a place like this?" he asked.

Justin shrugged, even though he knew full well the answer Ambrose was looking for was something along the lines of, *No, it's a terrible idea for me to work there.*

"It's just that with your, uh, history, I think that being in an environment like that every day might not be too healthy," he said.

By history, Ambrose meant the incident that got Justin sent away to the psychiatric hospital and the whole reason he was now required to meet with a caseworker each week to prove he was successfully reentering society.

"This is completely different," Justin said. "It's nothing like that at all. I explained all that. I got confused."

"Right," Ambrose said. "My concern is that working at a job like this might cause you to become *confused* again."

A voice in his head said, *He's saying confused, but what he means is crazy. He thinks you're looney tunes.*

"Well, it's really about selling products," Justin said. "That's how they make their money."

"It's not only the tarot cards," Ambrose said. "I mean, I'm not sure how comfortable I am with you having so much interaction with the public, even if it is just over the phone. What about that warehouse job I showed you last week? Did you submit an application?"

"I'm not really interested in that," Justin said.

It was the wrong answer, but it was the truth. Ambrose rubbed his eyes again.

"Virgil, I can't tell you not to take this job, but it is my strong opinion that this psychic hotline job is a bad idea."

Psycho hotline, said a voice only he could hear. *But he called you Virgil, and that's not who you really are. So he doesn't know anything. He doesn't know anything at all.*

"Shut up!" Justin screamed the words out loud and jumped up out of the chair.

Ambrose flinched before giving him a stern schoolmarm expression.

"Well," Ambrose said, "I think that today's session is now over."

"I'm sorry," he said. "I wasn't shouting at you."

"Well, there's only two of us in this room," the caseworker said.

"I know, I know," Justin said.

Ambrose's voice was gentler when he said, "Virgil, if you have this much difficulty having a short conversation like this, do you really think you're going to be able to handle talking to people on the phone all day long?"

~

J ustin retrieved his mail from the cluster of mailboxes just
outside his apartment and flipped through a stack of bills
and junk mail addressed to Virgil Chandler as he walked
to his front door, so he almost didn't notice the way one of his
neighbors, out walking a small dog, moved swiftly to get as far
away from him as she could.

He wasn't surprised that everyone wanted to keep their
distance from him, but it upset him. The injustice of it was
what hurt the most. All he wanted to do was help people. It
wasn't his fault the voices insisted on being obtuse. He longed
for clarity and an off button.

Yes, an off button would be very nice. That would prevent
things like his outburst earlier in Ambrose's office. No doubt
that was something that would get written up and added to his
file. As he watched the woman and her tiny dog scurry away, he
resisted shouting after her that he was harmless, that he'd just
been trying to help.

You're such a good helper. This time, at least, it wasn't one
of those voices from another realm, but a voice from his own
past that he heard in his head as he let himself into his apartment. The voice belonged to his mother. He missed her every
day, but most of all when he found himself all alone in his sad
little apartment.

Growing up, it had been just the two of them in that little
house on that busy road. They ran their business out of the
room at the front of the house and lived in the rooms at the
back. It hadn't been much, but in so many ways it had been
perfect.

His mom ran the show, and he was her helper. *You're such
a good helper.* It was his help that had made the business thrive,
but could he really take responsibility?

What he was supposed to do, what his mother had taught him to do, was to sneak around and go through the pockets and the handbags of the different customers who came in. He had been a small, quiet child. The clients barely noticed him. He was just a strange little boy scurrying around and playing with his toys while his mother told them the answers to all their burning questions.

The answers she told them came from the stuff Justin found, the little clues in their pockets and purses that helped his mother to give them a reading that would astound them and ensure that they came back again and again because they believed she was the real deal.

But pockets and purses didn't always have useful clues in them. Sometimes his mom was forced to improvise, and those readings never went as well. Justin learned he didn't need to rely on the clues he found in the customers' possessions. That was what his mother had taught him, but he found another way.

When he needed to find out useful information about a customer, he only had to tune in and listen to what the voices had to tell him. They told him what people were feeling and thinking. If they were scared or upset about something, the voices let him know.

More importantly, they told him clues about what things were going to happen to the customers in the future. Justin would deliver these messages to his mom, who would then pretend to have discovered this by looking at someone's palms or gazing intently into their eyes.

It was a system that worked well. Justin liked being able to give people helpful information by way of his mother. His mother liked being able to astound people with what they thought were her psychic powers. And the voices liked that they could use Justin to get their message out there. It all worked so well until that day Justin decided not to share what the voices had told him.

Up until then he had lived a good and happy life, but the day he decided he knew more than the voices was the day everything changed. After that, everything started to go wrong. The voices toyed with him, giving him confusing messages. He was powerless to help anyone, and whenever he tried, he ended up messing everything up.

That was why his neighbors all ran away when they saw him. That was why he had to go see a caseworker every week.

3

SAGE HAD NOT BEEN able to stomach coffee since his sister's murder. She was killed driving home from her shift at the coffee shop, and so he associated the beverage with her. His caffeine intake was limited to diet soda and tea. The truth was, even the smell of coffee made his stomach queasy, but he took his green tea back to the table PhillyFury had staked out at Culver Coffee and did his best to ignore the acrid aroma of roasted coffee beans.

"How did you find me?" Sage asked, still working at connecting this face in front of him with the forum posts he had read over the years.

PhillyFury shrugged. "It's what I do."

"Then I take it you know my name," Sage said.

"Sage Dorian," his companion admitted. "Formerly a detective on the Culver Creek police force."

"You've done your homework," Sage said. "I'm afraid that puts me at a disadvantage."

"Oh, sorry. Ambrose Radcliffe." He thrust out his hand, and Sage shook it.

"Ambrose," Sage repeated. "That's your real name?"

"Unfortunately," Ambrose said. "My mother thought it sounded rich."

Sage considered Ambrose's username.

"You live in Philadelphia?" Sage asked.

"I used to," Ambrose said. "I'm out in the suburbs now, lower Bucks County."

"That's a long way to drive for a cup of coffee," Sage observed.

"I needed to talk to you."

"You could have messaged me on the forum," Sage pointed out, then he wondered if maybe Ambrose had already tried that. It had been some time since Sage was active on the crime forums.

"I know," Ambrose said. He looked sheepish as he stared down into his coffee cup. "Some things have happened. I guess I just figured it would be better if I came out here in person, made sure it was really you."

"What things?" Sage asked. "And why me, exactly?"

"I thought maybe since you were a cop, you were the right one to go to. I'm not really sure who I can trust anymore."

In his line of work, Sage had seen his fair share of paranoia. Ambrose certainly sounded paranoid. It didn't really fit with the reasonable, measured tone Sage remembered from his forum posts. But sometimes people were different in real life from how they seemed online, and sometimes people changed. Sometimes things happened that changed people forever. He was a completely different person from who he had been before his sister's murder.

"Plus, you were one of the original ones on the case," Ambrose said, "back in the day."

On the case was how they used to describe it on the forums, when amateur sleuths put their heads together to try to solve a real-life crime.

"What case?" Sage asked.

"Remember the Unknown Suitor?" Ambrose asked.

That was the name they had given to a case concerning an unidentified man found murdered and burned beyond recognition inside a car.

"Vaguely," Sage said. "He was never identified, was he?"

"No," Ambrose said. "But there was some new interest recently. A new lead, I guess you could say."

Sage frowned, then took a sip of his green tea. He wondered what sort of new lead there could be for such an old case. Across from him, Ambrose sipped his coffee from a ceramic mug. Sage recalled the environmentalist bumper stickers on the back of Ambrose's Prius and felt bad about his own disposable paper cup.

"What sort of new lead?" Sage asked.

"You know about DNA-based genealogy, right?" Ambrose asked.

Sage worked hard at maintaining a poker face as he nodded.

"Right, well, there's been a certain contingent of web sleuths that have been going back through some old unidentified persons cases and using DNA genealogy to try and make an identification. It doesn't always work, but they've had some success."

"I take it you had luck with the Unknown Suitor," Sage said.

"Luck?" Ambrose laughed in a fake, nervous-sounding way and gave a rueful shake of his head. "This case is anything but lucky."

"But you were able to do a DNA test on this guy?" Sage asked.

Ambrose looked nervously around the small coffee shop like he was worried someone might be eavesdropping on them. This seemed unlikely in middle-of-nowhere Culver Creek, but Sage reminded himself until about ten minutes ago he himself had been feeling a bit itchy about someone in a silver car following him around.

"So I was wondering why you're no longer on the police force," Ambrose said.

"You don't trust me," Sage said.

"I don't trust anyone," Ambrose said. "It's nothing personal."

"Politics," Sage said. It was the short answer, and maybe not the complete story, but he wasn't about to tell this stranger about his experiences trespassing on the Pleasant Oaks Country Club, that had, for political reasons more than anything else, cost him his job.

"Right, well," Ambrose said. "The thing is, there was a group of us from the forum, we decided to form a task force to track down the identity of the Unknown Suitor and then hopefully the identity of whoever murdered him. We agreed to meet up in person at a place kind of like this." Ambrose waved his hand around at the coffee shop.

"Meet up in person?" Sage said. It was pretty much unheard of in the web sleuth forum. Ambrose was the first person Sage had ever met from the forums, and he had hung out there for years.

"Yeah, I know," Ambrose said. "The idea was we needed to go down to Maryland to get a DNA sample, then get it to a lab, but one of the forum regulars, CockatielOwner56, works at a lab that does DNA testing, and she wasn't that far away. Diane, aka DaddysLilGirl, joined us as well. Then there was Oaky. He lived up in the Poconos, and he's real good with analyzing maps and stuff. So he drove down."

Sage nodded absently, but the truth was he had stopped listening when Ambrose mentioned DaddysLilGirl. It was a handle he knew all too well.

"Well, we managed to go down and collect the sample, but then everything got weird," Ambrose said.

"Weird how?" Sage asked.

"Cockatiel, her real name is Penny. She was supposed to get the sample analyzed and get back to us, only she never contacted us, and when I called the lab to ask for her. They said she was missing. Said she hadn't shown up for work, and no one knew where she was. What the hell, right? So I try to get ahold of Oaky, and it turns out he got admitted to the hospital for a heart attack, and then ended up dying. I mean, he was kind of old, so that wasn't that crazy, but then I try to get ahold of Diane, and it's like she disappeared into thin air."

"She's missing too?" Sage asked.

"Yeah, I mean, I guess," Ambrose said.

Sage couldn't say he was disappointed to learn that DaddysLilGirl might have met with misfortune—karma and all that—but he was bothered by Ambrose's ambiguity.

"You haven't heard from her?"

"She flew here from out of state," Ambrose explained. "California. I tried her cell and get an out-of-service message. I tracked down the place where she works in California, or at least I thought I did, but no one there seems to know her."

Sage nodded.

"Don't take this the wrong way," Sage said, "but if I was meeting up in person with a bunch of people I only knew by way of a true-crime forum, I might use a fake name and a burner phone."

"No, I know," Ambrose said. "I thought the same thing." He looked down into his coffee mug. "It's just with Penny missing and Oaky dead, it concerns me that I haven't been able to get in touch with Diane."

"Did you report her missing to the police?" Sage asked.

"Tried to," Ambrose said. "They seem to be under the impression that she's some online girlfriend who ghosted me."

"So that's why you were following me around?" Sage asked.

"I thought since you knew me from the forums and because you used to be a cop that you could help." Ambrose reached into the pocket of his fleece jacket and pulled out some folded papers. There were maybe half a dozen sheets that had been folded in thirds, then again in half to fit into the pocket. Ambrose worked to smooth them out on the coffee shop table. "Ow!"

"Are you okay?" Sage asked.

"Paper cut." Ambrose pulled a cloth handkerchief from his pocket and held it to his bleeding finger. Sage was reminded of his grandfather, the last person he could remember who went around with a cloth handkerchief.

With his non-injured hand, Ambrose passed the papers to Sage. "These are our notes from the investigation," he explained. "After things got weird, I printed this stuff out and deleted everything from the web. You can keep those if you want. I've got another copy."

Sage looked down at the printouts. They looked to be Ambrose's own notes from the message boards rather than a printout of the full string of messages. Sage wasn't sure what to do with this. He wanted to help, of course, but from what Ambrose had said, he wasn't sure anything weird really was going on.

Sure, the two women who had been part of the little investigative team had suddenly gone incommunicado, but was that so surprising? Ambrose had a certain intensity to him that might put off some people, especially women who might not appreciate what they took as sexual advances. Hell, for all Sage knew, the guy had been sending the women inappropriate text messages or maybe following them around like he'd been tailing Sage.

"Look, if it's any consolation, I don't think there's anything to worry about," Sage said.

"Easy for you to say," Ambrose muttered. "Anyway, you might be in danger too, now that you've met with me." Ambrose shook his head and looked miserable and bewildered. Sage almost felt sorry for the guy. "I just thought since you used to be a cop, maybe you could help out somehow."

"I can have an officer come down," Sage said. "Would you want that? I can have him take a statement."

"A statement," Ambrose muttered. "What's that going to do?"

"I'll have the police look into things, okay?"

Ambrose nodded.

Sage pulled out his phone, but then thought better of it. He didn't want to make a call to the station in front of Ambrose. This was the sort of thing that would require an explanation, and it might be better handled in person.

"Can you sit tight for a few minutes?" Sage asked. "I've got to run down to the station. It's not far. I'll be right back."

"Sure," Ambrose said.

Sage stood up and finished the remainder of his tea.

"Just wait here," Sage said, then he dropped his empty cup in the trash and headed for the door.

On the sidewalk, he glanced back through the coffee shop window at the table, but Ambrose had gotten up. Sage spotted him at the trash can and frowned as Ambrose retrieved Sage's discarded tea cup from the trash. Ambrose pulled a plastic bag from his pocket and placed the cup inside it. Sage remembered the Sierra Club bumper sticker. Ambrose apparently took his environmentalist duties pretty seriously. If he had behaved in a similar way when meeting up with his fellow web sleuths, it could also explain why the others had stopped returning his calls.

4

"YOU PSYCHIC?" asked Lennie, Justin's new boss, and before
Justin had a chance to answer, Lennie continued. "Of course
you are. Everyone who works here says they're psychic. Bullshit. If you idiots were really psychic, you would win the
lottery, but no, you're working this crappy job."

Lennie strode briskly through a maze of cubicles while
Justin struggled to keep up. Around them a hundred different
phone conversations were taking place. Justin had been hearing
voices in his head since he was a kid, so he was good at dealing
with distractions, but even he was a bit overwhelmed by all the
chatter.

"Well, I'm not paying you to be psychic," Lennie said. "I'm
paying you to sell healing amulets and meditation crystals."

Lennie came to an abrupt stop, and Justin, who had been
busy paying attention to one of the phone conversations, nearly
ran into him. He looked up and saw that they had come to an
empty cubicle. His workspace, he realized.

"So," Lennie went on, "you just shuffle the cards, deal some
out, and tell them what it says."

He slapped a deck of tarot cards down on the empty desk, and Justin picked them up. Occasionally, his mother had done tarot readings, usually if someone specifically requested it, but that had never been her favorite thing. There was too much unpredictability in the cards. She had tried to subtly mark them, but even so, there was too much chance of error with card readings.

"I've never done—"

"A tarot reading?" Lennie finished. "Good! It proves you're not as weird as some of the freaks here. Don't worry, everything you need to know is on the cards."

Justin looked at the first card in the deck, then the next. The cards had been altered with taped-on pieces of paper that provided a short script about what to say regarding each card, and then below this were suggestions for the "healing energy" products they should try to pitch to each customer.

"The trick is to make them worried, but not too worried," Lennie said. "Convince them their situation is anything but dire, and if they just go ahead and order whatever product you pitch, everything's just going to be peachy keen."

Lennie slid open the top drawer of the desk and pulled out a laminated sheet of paper that he set down at the workstation. It was a listing of the different products they sold. There was a photo, a description and pricing information for each item.

Get a load of this tool, said a voice only Justin could hear. *Thinks he's hot shit because he's the manager, but if he was such hot shit, would his girlfriend be cheating on him with the UPS delivery driver?*

Justin fought to ignore the insidious voice, and Lennie mistook the look on his face for shock at the prices that were charged for healing amulets.

"I know what you're thinking," Lennie said. "Who's going

to pay $29.99 for some ugly-ass necklace, but what you have to keep in mind is these are some gullible bastards. I mean, they called some number for a free psychic reading, after all."

Marks. That was a term that some in the psychic trade used. But his mother had never been fond of such language.

Even though his mother wasn't gifted, even though she at first relied on the clues her young son was able to lift from the pockets and purses of her clients, she never looked down on the people who came to her for readings. She genuinely did want to help them.

Well, of course she wanted them to come back again and again. Repeat customers were good for her bank account, but Justin understood it was more than that. His mother honestly saw her psychic business as a way to give people comfort, hope and encouragement during trying times.

Her methods may not have been entirely aboveboard, but her mission was to help, not harm. Justin wasn't sure he could say the same about healing amulets or overpriced crystal sets. Then again, perhaps these talismans were, like his mother's readings, a way to help people get through trying times.

An amulet or a crystal didn't actually have to be magical in order to work. All that was required was that its user believed in its power to help them. That seemed to justify the pricing. Would people really believe a dollar store necklace could help them? Probably not, but they just might think a thirty-dollar healing amulet could ease their suffering.

"Any questions?" Lennie asked.

"What happens if the caller doesn't want to purchase an item?" Justin asked.

"Look, I'll be honest, a lot of them won't. They just want the free reading, but trust me on this, use the cards, stick to the script, and you'll sell plenty of junk."

It really wasn't all that much different from his mother's business. In her line of work, the people who made the best customers, the ones who came back again and again, were the ones facing some challenge that needed the balm her readings offered.

There were always those people who stopped by on a lark, but those were hardly ever the ones who became regulars. They saw getting a reading as entertainment. To them it was like going out to the movies.

That had been the case for the girl.

~

I t had been late on a Saturday night, and his mother was getting ready to close up shop when a car pulled into their little parking lot. Business had been slow that week, so his mother quickly flipped the Closed side back around to Open and went back to her post. Nodding for him to be ready.

Justin was eighteen, and his post was seated at the counter, where he explained the different types of readings and their rates and then processed payments. His mother said it was better if he handled the money stuff, since it seemed weird if the psychic was the one playing cashier. Never mind that in their operation, Justin was the real psychic. Anyway, having him be the one who handled payments gave him a reason for being present in the room.

When he had been a little kid playing on the floor, people hadn't questioned his presence, but it was different now that he was older. If he didn't have a specific job to do, it would have been strange for a teenage boy to just be lurking in the room during these very personal readings. As it was, he often ducked out of the room after he had done the payment transaction so that his mother could offer the illusion of giving a reading in complete privacy, never mind that Justin could hear every word that was said as he waited on the other side of the flimsy wall.

The thing was, after he had gotten the money and transmitted any important information about the customer to his mother, there was no need for him to be in the room, but he did need to be there to find out about the customer. The voices didn't bother to tell him things about people when he wasn't in their presence.

They had long since stopped relying on the inefficient pocket-snooping method, and instead relied exclusively on Justin's gifts, or rather what the voices decided to tell him. The way it worked was, as Justin was explaining the different services and rates, something he could and did do on autopilot, he listened to what the voices had to say about the customer. He would surreptitiously jot some notes down on a small piece of paper.

Then, once the customer was getting settled in the reading chair, Justin would casually hand off the note to his mother. It was a simple, well-honed, sleight-of-hand technique that no one ever seemed to pick up on.

The information would be spot-on, though not especially detailed, but that didn't matter. His mother worked best with a minimal amount of information. It actually made what she had to say more authentic-sounding. Being foggy or unclear on some points gave the illusion that she was a real psychic.

But the girl, Melodie was her name, didn't think his mother was a real psychic. She thought the whole thing was a scam, and it was all Justin's fault.

∼

"So what do you think?" Lennie asked, interrupting Justin's memory of the most beautiful girl he had ever met. "You ready to give it a go?"

"Now?" Justin asked. He had assumed there would be some sort of training he would have to go through.

"Well, that's what you're getting paid for," Lennie said. "Look, you'll be fine, Virgil. It's not rocket science."

5

SAGE HAD NOT BEEN BACK inside the station since his termination, and now he realized he wasn't sure how he felt about entering the building. His arrival would cause a scene, and that was the last thing he wanted. So he called Rod from outside.

His former coworker stepped out onto the sidewalk less than a minute later and appraised Sage with equal parts concern and fear. Sage tried to recall the last time he had showered. It had definitely been at least twenty-four hours, and he feared it might have been far longer than that. Time had ceased to have the same meaning for him since he became unemployed. His clothing couldn't be considered clean, and he really wished he had run a comb through his hair before going for what he thought was just going to be a stroll around the block.

"What's wrong?" Rod asked.

"Nothing's wrong," Sage said. It was a lie. Everything was wrong. "It's just, I need you to take a statement."

"Okay," Rod said, but he said it very slowly, like he was

talking to a child or a crazy person. He slipped a pad and a pen out of his pocket. "What happened?"

"No," Sage said. "Not from me. From a friend. Well, not a friend, but someone I know. I mean, we just met, but I've known him for a while online."

Rod looked confused. Sage wished he had planned out what he was going to say. He sounded like he was mentally ill.

Rod looked around.

"Where is he?"

"He's not here," Sage said. "He's waiting for me at the coffee shop. I told him I would come here and get you."

"Okay," Rod said again in that slow way. "You sure you're okay?"

"I'm fine," Sage said. "Look, I hadn't been planning on going out, just wanted to get some air, and then I ran into Ambrose, and well—if you've got a minute, can you walk down to the coffee shop with me?"

"Ambrose?" Rod asked.

"That's his name. His real name. He has a different user-name online, of course."

Rod still hadn't moved from just outside the station door, and Sage was feeling restless. He remembered how nervous Ambrose had been. He wasn't going to wait around that coffee shop forever. So Sage started to walk down the sidewalk in the direction of town, and Rod fell into step beside him.

"So he lives here," Rod said, "but you only knew him from online?"

"No, he lives out in Bucks County," Sage said. "Look, I should warn you that he's pretty nervous. He almost seems a bit paranoid, but that's because something happened. I mean, I don't even know if there was a crime that occurred, but I think it would make him feel a lot better if someone took down his statement."

"Something happened at the coffee shop?" Rod asked.

"No, nothing like that," Sage said. "It was just, see, he was working with these other people on an unsolved case, and—"

"He's a cop?" Rod asked.

"No, just an amateur detective," Sage said.

"What the hell's an amateur detective?" Rod asked. "Like the Hardy Boys or something?"

Sage hadn't anticipated having to explain the web sleuth forums to Rod. He wasn't sure the walk to the coffee shop would be long enough for that discussion.

"It's an internet thing," Sage said. "It doesn't really matter. The thing is, Ambrose is concerned because he can't seem to get in touch with the other people he was working with, and he's worried something happened to them. I mean, the one guy died, but the other—"

"Someone died?" Rod asked.

"Heart attack," Sage assured him, "natural causes. Look, the other two, they're both women, and I'm thinking maybe Ambrose creeped them out a bit, and that's why he hasn't been able to reach them."

"So he's a creep?" Rod asked.

"Not a creep, no," Sage said. "But maybe, you know, a little weird. Just do me a favor and take down his statement, and maybe we can look into the others from his group. Just to be sure."

"Sure," Rod said. They had reached the coffee shop door. "Let's go talk to Ambrose."

But Ambrose wasn't at the table. Sage remembered where he had last seen him, but Ambrose wasn't standing by the trash can to rescue items from the landfill.

"He's probably in the men's room," Sage said, but he had an uneasy thought. Had he seen Ambrose's Prius out front? He looked out the window, but the silver car was gone. The space was vacant. "I think he left." He pointed toward the window. "His car was parked right there. It was a silver Prius."

"You get the tag number?" Rod asked.

Sage realized he hadn't. What was wrong with him?

"I know how to get in touch with him," Sage said. "Online. I'll send him a message."

"Cool," Rod said. "Hey, it's good that I'm here. I could use a cup of coffee, and that swill at the station isn't really worthy of the name. You?"

"I'm good," Sage said.

"You sure? My treat," Rod said.

"I should probably get on home," Sage said.

"Sit with me for a bit," Rod suggested.

So a few minutes later, Sage found himself sitting at the same table, but this time with a new companion.

"How have things been going?" Rod asked.

"Fine," Sage said. "Good. I've been working on a project that I've been meaning to get to for a while."

"This would be investigating your sister's murder?" Rod asked.

Sage had never told Rod or any of his Culver Creek coworkers about that. So the question took him by surprise.

"I figured that's what you were doing at that country club," Rod said.

"Oh," Sage said.

"Look, I think what happened to you is complete bullshit."

"Thanks," Sage said.

"You think Senator Numbnuts had something to do with what happened to her?" Rod asked.

"I don't know," Sage said. "Maybe. She was secretly dating his son, but then she broke up with him. That was not too long before it happened."

"You think it was the son?" Rod asked.

"He wasn't in the country at the time," Sage said.

"Well, that's convenient, isn't it?" Rod said with a little snort. "You know these rich bastards don't do their dirty work themselves. They pay people to clean their houses and change their kids' diapers and whatnot, so when they want someone dead, they just pay someone to do that, too."

"It's a possibility," Sage admitted. But things had grown more complicated than he had first realized. It felt like his whole life was a lie, and he wanted so desperately to talk with someone about it, someone who would understand, but Rod wasn't that someone. No, the only person who could truly understand was his sister. That was why she had shown up at his dorm room that night, but when she had needed more than ever to talk to him, he had let her down.

"Seriously, man, are you okay?" Rod asked.

"I'm good," Sage assured him.

"You worried about this guy? This Ambrose fellow?"

Sage recalled how disarmed he had been when Ambrose stepped out of the car.

"No, he's fine," Sage said. "He seemed pretty nervous, though. I guess he just panicked and left."

"It's just with one of these online whackos," Rod said, "you know, you can't be too careful."

"He's fine," Sage said again.

"Does he know your address?" Rod asked.

Sage figured there was a good chance he did. Ambrose might have just worked out that Sage lived in Culver Creek because he had been on the police force. That information would have been easy enough to find without much digging. But the web sleuth crowd had little problem tracking down information that required a little more work.

"Probably not," Sage said. "But trust me, this guy is harmless."

"I'll walk back to your place with you just in case," Rod said.

"It's not necessary," Sage said.

"Yeah, I know it's not," Rod said, "but I miss working with you, and I'm in no hurry to get back to the station. Plus, my wife keeps telling me I need to get more exercise."

Sage shrugged. His lack of a shower and clean clothes was bad, but the state of his apartment was another matter entirely. Still, if he flat-out refused to let Rod walk with him back home, it would just look worse.

6

JUSTIN QUICKLY FELL INTO A ROUTINE. Answering phones, shuffling cards, reading scripts—it all became almost mechanical for him. Boredom set in.

He wasn't the only one bored. A little over a week into the job, the voices grew tired of telling him all his coworkers' secrets. As it happened, the workforce at the psychic sweatshop was not particularly thrilling, and their dull lives yielded little in the way of interesting tidbits. In their usual snarky way, the voices let him know they were displeased with the situation.

He ignored them, or tried to anyway, but one day while explaining to Rosalie in Peoria how the tiger stone beaded bracelet they sold could help her overcome her fear of flying so she could visit her sister down in Florida, the voices told him Rosalie should contact an exterminator about that sound she had heard coming from the attic. There were rats living up there, and they would soon chew through her wiring.

Justin broke off midway through his description of the tiger bead bracelet's benefits.

"Hello?" Rosalie said. "Are you still there?"

After another second or two of delay, Justin answered, "I'm here. Sorry about that."

He looked down at his laminated listing of products, found the text about the tiger bead bracelet. He tried to remember where he had left off, but before he could find his spot, the voice began to jabber away about how costly the damage to Rosalie's electrical system would be if she didn't get an exterminator in there in time.

"I think maybe there's something wrong with the connection," Rosalie said when he had gone silent again.

"Rats!" Justin blurted out. His voice was loud in their noisy office, and a hushed silence descended upon his fellow cubicle dwellers. He lowered his voice. "You have rats in your attic. They're going to chew up the wires if you don't hire an exterminator."

Then he ended the call, tore off his headset and dropped it on his desk. His heart raced as he stood up and stared at the discarded headset as if it were a live scorpion. Never in his life had the voices given him inside information on someone he was not in close proximity to.

Technically, it was too early for him to be taking his allotted fifteen-minute break, but he needed time to regroup and knew he would be useless taking another call right now.

J ustin sat on the battered old bench that overlooked the employee parking lot and beyond that a sad-looking municipal park. On another day, he might have thought the cold, bracing wind too chilly, but today it helped to restore his senses as he considered what had just happened.

He could now read people remotely, over the phone, unless maybe he couldn't. Maybe the voices were messing with him.

Wasn't it possible that Rosalie didn't have rats in her attic? She seemed like a nice woman, probably lived in a nice house. How would rats have gotten in there anyway? He had almost convinced himself it was all just a case of the voices pulling his leg with some nonsense about rats in an attic, but of course that couldn't be the case.

The voices could be obscure and cryptic. Sometimes they were angry and vindictive, but they always, in their own way, told him the truth. They didn't lie, and they didn't go in for pranks.

He had done the right thing telling Rosalie about the rat situation, but he had a problem on his hands. If the voices insisted on giving him information to share with every potential customer he spoke with, it was going to affect his ability to sell magic amulets and the like. Sure he could simply not share this information with the callers, but he knew all too well what happened when he didn't share the wisdom they imparted to him.

He could remember that night like it was yesterday. Melodie and her boyfriend showed up late, and they were all smiles and laughter as they stepped into the building. Clearly they didn't take this psychic thing seriously at all. Maybe one of them had dared the other to go inside. It was all just harmless fun for them.

Justin wasn't offended. He didn't really have the headspace to be offended. He was too busy falling in love. Melodie was the most beautiful girl he had ever laid eyes on. When she walked up to the counter and flashed her smile at him, it took his breath away.

It took him too long to remember to hand over their list of

services, and he stammered out an apology. Melodie and her boyfriend gave him a curious look. He could feel his mother's eyes burning a hole through his skull, but it was the voices that brought him back to reality, a hard, ugly reality that he wanted no part of.

Melodie's going to be killed. She's going to be murdered. He shook his head to dispel this unwelcome message, but the voices ignored his distress. *On her way home from work,* the voices continued. *She'll be driving home from work.*

He looked over at his mother with alarm, but of course she couldn't hear what the voices were saying. She nodded slightly at him, indicating that he should be jotting down his notes. He looked back at Melodie. She and her boyfriend now had their heads bent over the price list. They were still smiling, and she giggled as she whispered something to him.

Melodie's happy mood would vanish in an instant if his mother were to tell her what the voices had said, and Justin couldn't bring himself to be the cause of that smile leaving her face. Plus, what would be the point? The future forecasts the voices made always came true. Usually they were nothing as shocking and dire as this, though sometimes they did predict the death of a loved one.

Sometimes seeing a glimpse of the future could help people to better handle things or even get ahead of a bad situation, even if it didn't stop the bad thing from happening. That job they were considering applying for? Well, maybe they would now that the psychic had told them they were going to be fired from their present job. Those kind of readings were helpful, but what was helpful about knowing you were going to be murdered?

Maybe the information wasn't for her. Maybe the information was meant for him. There could be a way he could save her. But all he knew was her name, Melodie. It was a beautiful name to match a beautiful girl. Even when the voice whispered it in his head, it sounded lovely, and the voices never sounded lovely.

"Where do you work?" he blurted out.

Melodie and her boyfriend looked up at him in surprise. His mother made a noise as she sat at her little table.

"Sorry?" Melodie said in her dulcet voice.

"I, uh, I thought I recognized you from somewhere," he lied.

"Do you drink a lot of coffee?" she asked, the smile reappearing on her face. "I work at Pleasant Perk."

Of course he and his mother didn't frequent overpriced coffee shops. Business might have been good for her, but it was just enough to eke out a living. He shook his head. Melodie pointed at the listing for a basic reading on the price list, and he nodded as the boyfriend handed over cash.

He had to jot down his mother's note as he was making change. The truth was too unpalatable, so he wrote down made-up nonsense. He scribbled *trouble at home with parents, a change in her future, something bad happening at work*. It wasn't true, and it wasn't especially useful for his mother, but it didn't matter. Melodie wasn't going to come back for another reading anyway.

7

"I'VE BEEN KIND OF busy with things," Sage said when it was clear Rod wasn't going to just walk him to the door of his apartment and leave. "I haven't really been keeping up with the cleaning."

"What do I look like, Martha Stewart or something?" Rod asked.

"If I'd known you were coming . . ." Sage began.

"Yeah, yeah, you would've baked a cake."

Sage opened the door to his apartment, and he heard Rod's sharp intake of breath. His former coworker was careful not to say anything, but Sage had seen his reaction clear as day, and as he saw his apartment with fresh eyes, he couldn't really blame Rod. The place looked frightening.

Dirty plates and take-out containers did seem to be taking up most of the flat surfaces in the little apartment. What areas they hadn't commandeered were filled with the boxes he had sorted his sister's possessions into.

Then there were the Post-it Notes. His almost illegible scribbled notes were stuck up over all the walls. In some cases, notes were layered on top of one another two or three deep. He had spent hours arranging and rearranging the notes to try to make sense of things. That hadn't happened, but he had succeeded in transforming his apartment into a nightmare hellscape.

"Well, looks like Ambrose isn't here," Sage said.

"Really?" Rod asked. "How can you tell? I think a small army could be hiding out in here, and you wouldn't see them."

"I need to do some cleaning," Sage agreed.

"Or maybe just firebomb the place."

Sage was disappointed that Rod was showing no sign of leaving. It had been a mistake to allow him to come back here. He could see by the look on his former coworker's face that Rod was downgrading his assessment of Sage's mental health.

"I've been working," Sage said. "And there's not that much space."

Rod ventured into the apartment, watching his steps to avoid stepping on plates or pizza boxes. He went to a note-covered wall and just stared at it as if it was an art installation.

"So this is all for the investigation of your sister's murder?" Rod asked.

"You think I'm crazy," Sage said.

"Look, if one of my family members was murdered, and they hadn't caught the guy, I don't think I would rest until I tracked the bastard down either."

"Yeah, but I can see the look on your face," Sage said. "You think I'm crazy."

"I think maybe you need to get a job," Rod said. "The county parole office has an opening. It's not a great gig, I know, but maybe doing this investigation full-time isn't really such a hot idea." Rod pulled a note off the wall and squinted at it. "What does *ghost said related* mean?"

Sage came over and snatched the note out of Rod's hand. He folded it up and shoved it in his pocket.

"It's shorthand," Sage muttered.

Rod wandered over to Sage's table. It was home to a laptop and mounds of papers that had grown too tall and toppled into one another.

"Maybe you need to take a step back from this for now," Rod said.

"I'm not sure I can do that," Sage said.

Rod nodded. Then he scanned the messy, crowded apartment, his eyes taking in the alarming state of things.

"Look, I know I've got to do some cleaning," Sage said. "Once I get things straightened up, it won't be that bad."

"You need a hand?" Rod asked. "I could swing by after work."

"I've got it," Sage assured him. "Really. Don't worry."

But Rod still looked concerned. He picked up a piece of paper off the toppled stack closest to the computer. Sage saw what it was and quickly grabbed it out of Rod's hand.

"Right," Rod said. "Well, I guess I better get back to the station before they fire me too. If you have any issues with this Ambrose character, you call, okay?"

"You'll be the first to know," Sage said.

"And you can call me whenever," Rod said. "Even if you just want to talk to someone or whatever."

"Not necessary," Sage said, "but thanks."

Rod paused in the doorway like he was going to dispense some more words of wisdom, but then shook his head and departed with a wave.

8

"SO IT'S my understanding you had some trouble at work," Ambrose said.

Justin sat in the caseworker's office. He felt very out of it and disconnected. It was the same way the pills they forced him to take at the psych hospital had made him feel, but this time the feeling stemmed from his lack of sleep. Since the voices told him about Rosalie's rat infestation two days ago, he had barely gotten any sleep.

"It was nothing," Justin reassured him.

Ambrose pushed his reading glasses up on his nose and peered down at the papers in front of him.

"Became verbally abusive with a customer," he said, reading the notes that had been written there. Lennie had clearly exaggerated the situation.

"I was only trying to help her," Justin said, then he added a little fib to help his case. "Plus, she was hard of hearing, so I had to talk really loud to be heard. I guess it sounded like I was yelling at her."

He could have saved his breath. Ambrose clearly didn't believe him. He gave him one of his pitying stares.

"I think you'll recall I had some concerns about whether or not this was the right sort of job for you," he said.

"Am I being fired?" he asked.

"Well, no. I mean, that's not my decision to make. And apparently your employer said he spoke with you, and he believes you understood what you did was wrong."

"Yes," Justin said. He recalled the long talk Lennie had given him. A lot of blah, blah, blah and all about how you had to stick to the cards and stick to the script and everything would be fine. Yeah, right.

Justin knew all too well what happened when you ignored the voices, when you refused to impart to others what they considered to be valuable information.

"The customer will call back," Justin said.

"What?" Ambrose said.

"The customer, Rosalie, the one I yelled at. She'll call back, but not to complain. She'll be a good customer."

"Well, that remains to be seen," Ambrose said with a sigh.

"No, I know," Justin said.

"Oh, I see, this is one of your psychic visions, is it?"

He had once tried explaining to Ambrose that what he had were not visions, that he never saw anything, merely heard information, but clearly that had not sunk in. People were so married to the idea of seeing the future as opposed to hearing it.

But anyway, this prediction of his wasn't rooted in anything he had heard from the voices. He knew Rosalie would be a repeat customer because he had seen it all the time as a kid helping his mother. Give someone true and useful information about the future, no matter how vague, and they would become a customer for life. It was the "for life" bit that filled him with sudden, overwhelming sadness.

For life. It turned out his mother's customers for life weren't customers for all that long, and it was all because of Melodie Dorian. Because the night she walked into his life, the night he passed a note filled with some random lies to his mother, was the night everything in Justin's life started to go wrong.

It would have been one thing if the voices simply stopped speaking to him. He would have missed them, and it might have taken him some time to adjust to a life without their tidbits of knowledge, but in time it was something he might have appreciated. Most people didn't have voices whispering secrets in their ears all day long. For once, he could have lived a more normal human experience. Alas, this was not the way things went for him.

The voices did not stop speaking. If anything, they spoke to him even more. After he refused to share their message about Melodie, they grew angry with him, and they chose to make their displeasure known by filling his head with nearly nonstop chatter, but the tone and quality of their chatter changed.

Before, when they imparted their wisdom it was in a clear, no-nonsense way, but suddenly all that changed. Although technically they were still telling him the truth, the riddles and deliberately obtuse way of stating things made it feel like lies.

Almost immediately the business began to suffer as a result, and his mother thought it was all Justin's fault.

Late one night after they had closed up shop for the evening, his mother stood in his bedroom doorway waving a small square of paper at him. It was the note he had written for her regarding Mrs. Apostolos, one of their regular customers. It read "a large bird will speak to her."

This was the only sense he had been able to find in the

chatter, but *sense* might have been a generous term because the words had the feel of nonsense. Large, talking birds were not a regular occurrence in the Philadelphia suburbs.

"Is this your idea of teenage rebellion?" his mother asked. "Is that what this is about? Couldn't you just listen to loud music or steal from the liquor cabinet?"

"We don't have a liquor cabinet," he answered.

With all the chatter going on in his head, it was difficult to focus on things. He had hoped to burrow under his covers and go to sleep, but both the voices and his mother seemed determined to prevent this from happening.

"Don't get smart with me! And no more notes like this, do you hear me? I don't want to read anything else about large talking birds or winged waitresses or someone taking a trip to Uranus."

His mother was referring to other notes he had passed to her recently, notes that were directly transcribed from the strange, cryptic messages the voices had given him. He had hoped that when his mother shared this information with clients, they would understand immediately, but this had not been the case. Instead, his mother's clients seemed to be growing increasingly uneasy with her readings.

"I can't help it," he said.

"I don't know what you're playing at," she said, "but this business is what keeps a roof over your head and puts food in your mouth. You keep pulling this kind of crap and we'll both be suffering, do you hear me?"

He nodded. They couldn't go on like this. Fortunately, he knew exactly what had upset the voices. Now, he just needed to fix things. He needed to find Melodie.

9

THE SAME DAY Sage lost his job, an innocent-looking piece of mail arrived that shattered his world. Compared to that, getting fired was more like a small setback.

He picked up that piece of mail, the paper he had pulled out of Rod's hand only a few minutes earlier. Likely that had been an overreaction. Rod probably wouldn't have known what to make of the somewhat cryptic information. He probably would have been as in the dark as Sage was when he found a similar piece of paper while sorting through his sister's possessions.

The truth was, if a local resident hadn't had the DNA testing kit she ordered stolen by a porch pirate, he might never have figured out what the document his sister had from some place called Human History really was. But the universe had given him a clue, and he followed up on his hunch, and now he had a piece of paper in his possession that confirmed that his dad was not his biological father.

And now he had a pretty good idea of what his sister had been going through the night she showed up unexpectedly at his college dorm room. She had found out the truth years before he did, and because he had been too absorbed with his own unimportant problems to pay any attention to her, she had taken this information to the grave with her.

His phone vibrated on the table beside him. He glanced at the display and saw an incoming call from his mother. He half expected the phone to burst into flames. It had been nearly two weeks since he last spoke to his mother. She called every few days like clockwork.

He wasn't a complete monster. He had sent a few texts to let her know he was still alive, making vague excuses about being busy with work. So far he had not told either of his parents about his dismissal. But that was not the only reason he was avoiding speaking to his mother.

The other reason was staring him in the face—his report from Human History. Because his mother most certainly was already well-acquainted with the information it contained. He was angry with her for keeping this from him for all these years, but he was also a little scared.

Would someone who had held on to a secret for so long be willing to kill to ensure that such information never got out? It was ludicrous to think his mother had killed Melodie, absolutely bonkers. Even on the web sleuth forums, when theories were put forth that a family member might have murdered Melodie, suspicion only ever fell on him or his father. No one ever theorized that his mother was the killer.

Of course, most of the web sleuth forum threads that speculated a family member had murdered Melodie were dominated by one poster. That individual seemed convinced that Sage had murdered his sister. Her posts put forth an all too plausible theory that he was the killer, and she had succeeded in convincing many of the forum members that this was the most likely scenario. Just thinking about it disgusted him. The old anger welled up inside of him.

In his darker moments, he used to fantasize about tracking down that web sleuth, and after telling her she was a vicious monster that did not deserve to draw breath, he would force her to publicly recant her erroneous theories. Sometimes in this fantasy of his, he visualized himself crushing her computer beneath the wheels of his car so he could block her from accessing the message boards. These thoughts were just a way of easing the pain all those forum posts had caused him, and the truth was, he hadn't really thought about that revenge plan in a long time, not until Ambrose had mentioned that he was working with Sage's old online nemesis, DaddysLilGirl.

Sage picked up the papers Ambrose had given him. Case notes on the old Unknown Suitor mystery—that was what they had dubbed the unidentified victim's murder. As a younger man, still mourning the murder of his sister, Sage had been sucked into the case. Like his fellow web sleuths, he had been enthralled by the mystery. What was the identity of the man who had been murdered? And why had his killer gone to such great lengths to conceal it?

If Ambrose was correct, then his little ragtag team was close to identifying the victim, and if Ambrose's concerns were more than just paranoia, then somebody really wanted to make sure the victim's name stayed hidden. Even as he knew he needed to focus on his mission to find Melodie's killer, he could feel his old web sleuth instincts tingling. The Unknown Suitor case was a juicy one, and Sage longed to take another stab at it.

But his phone vibrated again, and this time it wasn't his mother.

10

THE VOICES soon let him know that what happened with Rosalie was no fluke. They were quite content to give him all sorts of unwanted insights into the lives of the phone-in customers. But Lennie had made it very clear that Justin wouldn't have a job anymore if he did not stick to the script. Unfortunately, there was no way to explain this to the voices. Though they loved to chatter away, they seemed to be deaf to anything he had to say.

So what was Justin to do? Ignore the voices and risk their wrath? He didn't like that idea one bit. So he did more or less stick to the script, but with certain extra little tidbits thrown in.

Take Joe, for example. Justin was reasonably sure that was not the real name of the guy who called in. He was a younger guy who wanted advice about a woman he had developed feelings for, a coworker of his. Justin shuffled the cards, and The Hermit card came up. So he gave Joe the scripted answers about his fear of loneliness and a warning to not be too self-absorbed at the risk of pushing his potential mate away.

But interspersed with these scripted statements, Justin did his best to impart the wisdom the voices had shared with him.

"One way to stave off loneliness," Justin said, "is to reach out to loved ones. For example, perhaps you have some relatives you haven't spoken to recently, a grandmother maybe."

"It's not really that I'm lonely," Joe said. "I guess I just really like this girl, and I don't know how to make her see that."

"Right," Justin said. "Well, sometimes women appreciate someone who is close to their family members. Your grandmother, for example. You should take your grandmother out for lunch sometime. That would impress that girl you like, I'm sure of it."

"Uh, okay, but I was thinking about maybe just buying her some flowers or something."

"Well, speaking of buying things, I wanted to tell you about our Sacred Love candle. Burn this candle for a few minutes each night to help bring love into your life."

"Yeah, I don't know if—"

"It's made with the highest quality essential oils, and it has been infused with mystical charms. Similar candles sell for fifty dollars or more, but this candle, which is like your own personal love potion, can be yours for just $19.99."

Justin heard the telltale click of the phone hanging up. A heavy sigh escaped his mouth.

"No worries, kid, you'll get the next one." Justin looked up to see Lennie passing through the cubicle maze. "That Sacred Love candle is always a tough sell."

But the lost candle sale wasn't what had brought on feelings of despondency. Justin was worried he hadn't sold the grandmother thing hard enough. He didn't want to come right out and tell Joe his grandmother was going to die, and he would be overcome by feelings of regret if he didn't reach out to her.

Would Joe take her out to lunch as Justin suggested, or at the very least give her a call?

Well, it was all out of Justin's hands now, and thankfully it was two minutes until quitting time. He had not counted on just how emotionally draining this job would turn out to be, and he began to wonder if Ambrose had been right about the job being too much for him. Maybe he should have taken that warehouse gig.

J ustin was still thinking about dying grandmothers and unheeded warnings as he pulled out of the call center's parking lot that evening, and he must not have been paying attention. The blare of a too-loud horn fixed that. He came to with a start and saw a large county bus barrel past. He shook his head at the irony of the whole thing. What a strange, strange world they lived in. And he was back to thinking about unheeded warnings again, but this time one from years ago.

He remembered he and his mother in that sad little kitchen of theirs eating breakfast together. The voices had kept him up half the night chattering in that nonsensical way that was how they presently communicated with him. He had tried as hard as he could to make some sense of what they were saying, had even taken out a piece of paper and written down all the words, as if maybe seeing them on paper would make everything clear.

"A nighttime hike is a perilous prospect for a woman who cannot see so well in the dark."

It sounded like the sort of thing one might get in an annoying fortune cookie. What did it even mean? The only part he was sure of was that his mother must be the woman it referred to. She was the only one around when Justin received the message, so it followed it must be about her, for this was long before the voices had taken to telling him about people on the other end of telephone lines.

But hiking? When had his mother ever hiked anywhere? And why would she be going for a hike in the dark?

"Are you planning on going away somewhere?" he asked her. "Like on a vacation?"

"Fat chance," his mother said with a little snort of a laugh. "With the way business has been lately, we're barely getting by. I certainly can't afford to go on any lavish vacations."

"What about a not-so-lavish one?" Justin asked. "Like camping or something, or hiking in the woods."

His mother didn't even bother to answer that. She just made a face at him like he was a lunatic and took a swig of her orange juice.

"Just don't go on any moonlit hikes, okay?" Justin said.

"I'll keep that in mind," his mother said and rolled her eyes.

So if his mother wasn't planning on going hiking anytime soon, what was with the weird warning? Justin brooded as he ate his breakfast without tasting it.

Maybe he had it all wrong. The voice might not be talking about his mother at all. He thought of the other thing that had been gnawing away at him. Didn't it make sense that the warning was really about Melodie? She was the one who was in danger at night, and this was just the voices' way of reminding him about that. After all, that was what they were so angry about.

"I need to borrow the car tonight," Justin said.

"What, you have a hot date or something?" his mother asked, but she was being sarcastic. She knew her homebody son didn't have any social life to speak of.

"Kind of," Justin said. "There's someone I need to go see."

This caused her to raise her eyebrows at him, but she shrugged.

"Suit yourself," she said. "I don't need it. I'm not going anywhere."

But she was wrong.

11

SAGE WAS SURPRISED to see a call coming in from his mother's neighbor. He wouldn't have put it past his mother to borrow the neighbor's phone just to trick Sage into picking up. On the other hand, it could very well be an emergency.

"Mr. Felton?" Sage asked, half expecting to hear his mother's voice.

"Sorry to bother you," Mr. Felton said in his raspy, old man voice. "I tried to call your mother, but it went to voicemail, and I had some concerns."

"What's wrong?" Sage was sure his mother was fine. She had just called him a few minutes ago.

"Maybe nothing," Mr. Felton said. "It's just, well, I saw this car kind of lurking about, and I didn't recognize it. It's not anyone here in the neighborhood."

"It's probably nothing," Sage said.

"Well, that's what I was hoping too," Mr. Felton said, "but then I saw it pull into your driveway."

He meant, of course, Sage's mother's house. A car in the

driveway was hardly cause for alarm. Maybe his mother had invited a friend over.

"I'll look into it," Sage promised Mr. Felton.

"Good, good, because it's a quiet neighborhood. We don't want any sort of trouble."

Maybe Sage was being paranoid, but did it sound like Mr. Felton was implying that the Dorians were the sort of family that brought trouble to the neighborhood, what with Melodie getting murdered and all that? It was probably for the best that Mr. Felton had ended the call, because Sage was thinking of delivering a nasty retort.

He now expected the voicemail his mother left to be her telling him how she had invited so-and-so over to the house, and maybe even suggesting he should stop by for a visit. But as soon as he began to play the recording, he could tell that wasn't the case. He could hear the clatter of noise in the background. His mother was out in public somewhere. In a resigned voice, she said, "Hi, it's Mom. Just calling to chat. Call me back when you get a chance."

Guilt weighed down on him. *Call her*, said a little voice in his head, but he wasn't ready for that. Not yet.

Instead, he grabbed his keys and his jacket. It would take him all of five minutes to call his mother and report that Mr. Felton saw a suspicious vehicle in the driveway. It would take him the better part of an hour to drive there and check things out in person. Probably the car would be long gone by then. His whole plan was unreasonable, but he trotted downstairs and got in his car. Perhaps he was just using any excuse he could to get out of his apartment. The place was starting to feel like a prison cell.

S age saw the car pull out of his mother's driveway just as he turned the corner. He saw a flash of silver as the little compact car headed down the road, and he wondered if he should pursue the vehicle or check to make sure the house was secure.

He slowed to a crawl as he drove past the house, eyeing the building for signs of damage, but everything looked okay. Maybe they had broken in through the back. The fence would have shielded the thieves or whoever they were from Mr. Felton's prying eyes.

"Detective Dorian?"

Sage looked up and saw a woman striding across the front lawn toward him. His mother's former real estate agent, Zoey Wilson. But Sage glanced toward the front door and saw the lockbox attached to the knob. Apparently his mother had put the house back on the market and rehired Zoey as her real estate agent. He was upset with her for not bothering to tell him this pertinent information, then remembered he was the one who hadn't returned any of her calls.

Sage pulled his car up to the curb. Though not strictly prohibited, parking in the road was frowned upon in this neighborhood, and Sage smiled to himself thinking about how this was just the sort of thing that might get Mr. Felton's goat.

"Doesn't want any trouble," Sage muttered as he exited the vehicle. "I'll show him trouble."

"Your mom's not here right now," Zoey said when she met him in the driveway beside her car, probably the same one Mr. Felton had deemed suspicious. That or the silver compact car he had just seen, which probably belonged to some prospective house buyers.

Zoey looked different since he last saw her. She had gotten a new haircut, and her clothing was different—brighter, cuter.

He realized he was gawking and did his best to recover his senses.

"Did you have a showing?" Sage asked.

"Yeah," Zoey said, "but I wouldn't get your hopes up. I think the place is out of their budget."

"So they just came here to hunt for ghosts?" Sage knew his mother chose Zoey as an agent because she specialized in haunted houses. It had caused a bit of friction between he and his mother.

"Well, that's not really what I focus on anymore," Zoey said. "I decided to rethink my whole business model, I guess."

It was understandable. A couple of weeks ago, in his last official act as a member of the Culver Creek police force, Sage arrested Zoey's sister Arielle after she murdered Zoey's boyfriend and attempted to kill Zoey. That kind of thing could shake someone up. In Sage's case, it led to his obsession with the web sleuth forums and his decision to go into law enforcement. For Zoey, apparently it led to her following a more traditional plan when it came to selling houses.

"There's no for-sale sign out front," Sage said.

"Yeah, we only just relisted it," she said. "This was the first showing. I still need to get the sign up."

"The neighbors were concerned when they saw strange cars," Sage said. "Or at least one of them was." He glanced across the road at Mr. Felton's house and wondered if the old geezer was spying on them right now.

"Oh, sorry," Zoey said. "Is that why you drove over here? I didn't mean to cause any problems."

"It's fine," Sage reassured her.

"It's just, I know your mother mentioned you were really busy with work," Zoey said.

Sage wondered if his mother had also mentioned that Sage wasn't returning her phone calls. He wouldn't put it past her.

He heard the approach of a racing engine, and they both looked up in surprise. It was an unusual sound on this quiet, suburban street, and Sage couldn't help but think of Mr. Felton across the road. It was a banner day for the neighborhood busybody. The car turned the corner and came into view, fishtailing due to the high rate of speed. The metallic silver paint caught the sun, and Sage was reminded of the car he had seen earlier, but this sedan was larger than the little compact.

Sage squinted at the vehicle. In the bright sunlight, he could just make out the shadowy figure of the driver, a baseball cap pulled down low. Then movement caught his eye.

"Look out!" he yelled.

He didn't have time to analyze what he was seeing, and Zoey didn't seem to realize what was going on. Instincts took over. He charged at her, knocking her backward onto the front lawn less than a second before something heavy crashed into the driveway. The car engine raced as it sped off down the road. He realized he had all his weight on Zoey, and he shifted his weight to his elbow.

"You saved my life," she said in a stunned, dazed voice. She reached her hand up and ran it through his hair, and he flinched. He remembered now that it had been at least a day since he showered and probably even longer than that since he had run a comb through his hair. It must be in a serious state of disarray.

He caught her hand in his. It was so small and soft. Heat rushed through him. It was more than just his embarrassment over being a big, unwashed oaf. This was something else entirely, and he was suddenly conscious of how much of his body was pressed against her.

"I'm sorry," Zoey stammered, and she made a move to sit up.

"For what?" he asked.

What happened next was pure instinct. The animal part of his brain took over. He leaned his face closer to hers, and their lips met. The kiss was brief, but electric. They both sprang back from it at once. It was his turn to mutter an apology.

They untangled their limbs and got back to their feet.

"Are you okay?" he asked.

She nodded. He followed her gaze and saw the brick that had landed in the driveway. Her car, at least, had been spared.

"I think there's a note," she said. She went to reach for it, but he was quicker and snatched up the brick. He tossed the brick onto the grass after he removed the attached piece of paper. He held it, still folded, as he looked down the road, but the car was long gone.

"It's probably just one of those curiosity-seeker types," Sage said. "This is the kind of stupid stunt they'd pull."

"We could have been killed," Zoey said.

Sage opened up the piece of paper and stared at the single word written there. Ironic, in light of what Zoey had just pointed out.

"What's it say?" Zoey asked.

He shoved the slip of paper in his pocket even though what he wanted to do was destroy it. Who was it intended for? He felt a chilly, prickly sensation. How would anyone have known he would be here? The most likely target was his mother, but meeting Ambrose earlier and hearing about his old nemesis DaddysLilGirl had sent his mind to a dark place and dredged up some old wounds.

The single word written on the piece of paper was *MURDERER*.

"You sure you're okay?" Sage asked. She nodded. "Well, then you probably need to get going. I do too."

"You just got here," she pointed out. "Your mom should be

back in a few minutes. She said she was just going to hang out in a coffee shop until the viewing was done."

But Sage was in no shape to talk to his mother right now.

12

JUSTIN TOOK a moment between calls to glance around at his fellow coworkers and marvel at just how adaptable he was. He had adapted to being orphaned, to living another man's life, and now to a constant barrage of chatter each time he spoke to a customer on the phone. Someone with less fortitude might have crumbled under the pressure, and though it was a bit over-whelming at first, he had found his stride. Now he had no problem answering the calls, reading the script and inter-spersing whatever nuggets of wisdom the voices insisted he impart.

He felt a bit in awe of his own skills. Lennie had just publicly praised him for being the top earner last week, and looking over at the big dry-erase board where they tracked sales stats, he could see he was on target to be top earner again this week. Things were going good. Some might say too good.

"I'm concerned about my son," said the next woman who called in. "He hasn't spoken to me in weeks."

"That must be difficult for you," Justin said in a kind, sympathetic voice.

"Oh, it is," she said.

"Let me consult my sources and see what sort of help they can provide," Justin said.

He dutifully shuffled the deck and turned over the top card, Temperance.

"Hmm," he said speculatively, as if he was discerning some meaning from the cheap card with its taped-on notes. "Well, this may not be what you want to hear," he said. The voices began to chatter noisily, but he ignored them for now. "But my sources advise you to be patient. Your son may not be speaking with you right now, but he will. The thing is, you must give it time. It will do no good to force the issue."

She's in danger! She's in grave danger! The voices were now screaming at him. It was all Justin could do to tune them out, and just a minute ago he had been thinking about how he was such a master at this whole business. There was a danger in being overly confident. *Hospital! She's going to be taken to the hospital.*

"I'm worried about him," she said. "He's all I have left. His sister was killed several years ago, and it's really had a terrible impact on all of us. Recently he's become more obsessed with what happened to her."

"I'm sure your son will reach out to you when he's ready, Mrs.—" He paused because he realized he didn't know the woman's name. *She's keeping a secret*, the voices said in the silence. *That's why the son won't speak to her.*

"Dorian," the woman said. "Kelly Dorian."

For a moment, the world stopped spinning. It was the point in the phone call where Justin was supposed to switch into salesman mode and sell her whatever magic charm was going to help her with her troubles. They had an amulet to assist with wayward children and a crystal set to aid with communication difficulties. Both would have been good fits for Kelly Dorian's dilemma, but Justin wasn't thinking about amulets or crystals. All he was thinking about was Melodie Dorian, and he seemed to no longer have the ability to speak.

"I'm sorry," he said. "I have to go."

He ended the call abruptly, jumped up from his desk and ran to the bathroom. The voices shouted in his head the whole way. Why hadn't he warned her about her danger? Why hadn't he said anything about the secret that had come between her and her son? But shouldn't the voices have known better than anyone why Justin was so upset?

He just about made it to the bathroom stall before throwing up his lunch. He squatted there on the tile floor, his head pressed against the cool metal of the stall divider as sweat poured out of him.

J ustin had felt a weird prickly feeling the night he had stepped out of the house and gotten into the driver's seat of his mother's car. He mistook it for nervousness. Because he was exceptionally nervous.

He had never had a girlfriend and barely had what could be considered friends. Being the strange, moody son of a road-side psychic was not exactly a ticket to high school popularity. In just a couple of months he would graduate, and he was looking forward to the event because it meant he would never have to endure another minute of school. He had no college plans, and the truth was, no plans at all.

Maybe that was weird for someone with psychic gifts, but as forthcoming as the voices were about the lives of everyone he came in contact with, they never told him about his own life. His future was not something he had given much thought to. He had idly entertained the idea of getting some sort of job and saving up money to do some traveling. He thought he might like that—traveling around and seeing different places. It felt like something that would be fun and exciting.

But was he being realistic? For someone who was now exceptionally nervous just to drive across town and go into a coffee shop he had never stepped inside of before, was it even remotely possible he could actually handle traveling to some faraway place without becoming overcome by crippling nervousness?

These thoughts about traveling seemed to stir up the attention of the voices, who were still prattling on about his mother and her alleged hike in the dark. But he had already delivered that message to his mother. He wanted to shout at the voices to shut up, but he was alone in the car, still parked in the driveway, and to do so would only make him look crazy. So he turned on the car, cranked up the radio to drown out the chattering voices and drove across town.

Five minutes later, he was sitting in his mother's parked car in the Pleasant Perk parking lot trying to work up the courage to go inside. It was late, and he knew the coffee shop would be closing soon. He didn't even know if Melodie would be there, but if she was, what would he say?

Would she recognize him from when she came in for her reading? He wouldn't count on it. People tended to have their mind on other things when they stepped into the shop. But if she did recognize him, would she be weirded out that he showed up here? It was a public place, and he could say he just stopped in for some coffee, but, no, that was no good.

He had to tell her. He had to deliver the warning the voices wanted him to. Maybe then they would stop with all their cryptic messages about dangerous nighttime hikes.

Too much time passed. He switched the car on long enough to consult the clock. Almost an hour had gone by.

No more dithering. He would go inside, but first he pulled down the visor and checked his appearance in the mirror there. He wasn't happy about his hair. Finger-combing it only made it worse. He scrounged around in the messy backseat and turned up an old baseball cap. It did the business of hiding his messy hair, and it might also make it less likely that Melodie would recognize him.

Maybe then he wouldn't seem so creepy. Well, that would only last until he opened his mouth and delivered his warning. As soon as he told her that her life was in danger, he was going to look like the creepiest creep who ever creeped.

He punched the steering wheel in frustration. Then he remembered he was in a brightly lit public parking lot. He looked around and noticed that the lot had mostly emptied out. Then everything grew dimmer. He looked toward the building and saw that the interior lights had been shut off. He was too late. A second later, the front door opened, and he saw her. Melodie. She was as beautiful as he recalled. She turned his way, and she seemed to be looking straight at him.

Then a cacophony like he had never heard before started up. Instinctively, he clapped his hands over his ears to drown out the sound, but it did nothing. The noise was coming from inside his head.

13

IN MOST MURDER INVESTIGATIONS, the victim's identity is known and it's only the murderer who needs to be discovered. But occasionally even the victim's name is unknown.
That was the case with the man who would come to be known
as the Unknown Suitor.

It was 1:22 in the morning when patrolman Keith Ewing
saw a strange fiery glow in the distance. He radioed in to the
dispatcher that he was headed down a dirt driveway to take a
closer look. What he found was a vehicle engulfed in flames.
Minutes later, the volunteer fire department in the western
Maryland town were on the scene. They were able to extin-
guish the flames but could not save the car's sole occupant. The
body was burned beyond recognition.

Patrolman Ewing's fears that he had not acted quickly
enough to save the unidentified man were soon dispelled by a
coroner's report that found a bullet hole in the man's skull, and
coupled with the fact that the man's body was found in a seated
position behind the steering wheel of the car, the coroner

concluded that death had occurred before the vehicle ever caught on fire.

Police would determine that the car was reported stolen three days earlier in Harrisburg, Pennsylvania. They had less luck with the burned man.

Dental records were compared to known missing-persons cases with no success. Police waited anxiously for someone to report their neighbor, friend, relative or employee had disappeared, but it seemed the man burned in the stolen car found in a remote driveway was not missed by anyone.

It was the sort of puzzling mystery that caught the attention of amateur web sleuths. Finding a killer was not always an easy task, but it was that much more difficult when the victim's identity was unknown.

The mystery man could have been anyone. He might have been just a drifter or drug addict who had crossed paths with the wrong person. In which case the killer would most likely never be charged with this crime.

The web sleuth crowd decided a key to understanding who the dead man was and what happened to him was one of the few pieces of evidence that had been recovered from the burned car. Found near the man's corpse was an item that had possibly been held in his pants pocket before his clothing was destroyed in the fire, a woman's diamond ring.

The plain ring coupled with the small stone made the amateur sleuths surmise that it was likely an engagement ring purchased by a young man for his intended fiancée. Since police estimated the unidentified man to be somewhere between eighteen and twenty-five years old, the web sleuths dubbed him he Unknown Suitor.

But who was his intended bride, and why had she not come forward? Some theorized there might be another body out there the police should be looking for. Others wondered if the killer might have abducted the young woman.

Though it made for a wonderfully tragic love story, Sage had always had a problem with these theories. One young person that nobody on earth seemed to be looking for, he could accept, but the likelihood that there could be two different young people that nobody seemed to be looking for and that they were in love seemed pretty slim. Unless they had met at a homeless shelter, Sage didn't see how this could be possible.

He had always believed the story was far less romantic. In his mind, he had seen the Unknown Suitor as a scorned suitor. He had proposed to the girl of his dreams, only to be turned down. Maybe he hadn't even had the opportunity to propose. She had dumped him for some other guy before he even popped the question, and he was left with a useless ring and a broken heart.

Perhaps he was so crushed he turned to drugs or went on a drinking binge that had somehow ended up with him getting a bullet in his head. Had his intended's new boyfriend been involved in the Unknown Suitor's demise? That was a theory that had been batted around in the message boards back in the day. It was all speculation, though.

Now, with the benefit of time and a career as a police officer, Sage saw a far less romantic possibility to the whole affair. The Unknown Suitor was likely no suitor at all. The ring was probably stolen. That sort of crime was nearly always some desperate drug addict trying to score his next fix. Most likely, in his desperation the Unknown Suitor had ripped off the wrong person and paid the price with his life.

Sage felt a little sad to have grown so jaded and cynical in a relatively short span of time. He missed the younger version of himself who was still willing to believe in a romantic, if tragic, backstory for an unidentified dead man.

That younger version of himself was still there, buried beneath layers of protective hardness. He knew because it was that youthful version of himself that had been woken from its slumber when he brashly kissed Zoey Wilson on his mother's front lawn. And in the intervening day and a half, that younger, idealistic *him* had entertained the idea of calling Zoey before the cynical man he had become quashed that idea.

What would be the point in calling Zoey? He didn't need anything like that in his life, and the last thing Zoey needed was a broken wreck of a man like him. Hadn't the woman been through enough?

She saw Melodie. Sage ignored the little voice in his head. Sure Zoey claimed to have seen Melodie's ghost after she had been shot, but she had lost a lot of blood and was slipping out of consciousness. It was nothing but a hallucination brought on by the trauma she had suffered. Proof of that was the message she had delivered from his dead sister: "You're related."

At the time, the comment had seemed ludicrously obvious. Of course he and his sister were related. But that was before he learned he and his father were not related. He believed that shortly before her death, Melodie learned that she too was not related to their father, but what if Sage had it all wrong? What if Sage was the only illegitimate member of their family? Of course, he and Melodie would still be related, but not as closely related as they had always thought. Was that what Melodie had found out right before she was killed?

He reminded himself that he was obsessing over a message from a non-existent ghost. All kinds of things caused people to hallucinate. That didn't make them prophets. And so he talked himself out of calling Zoey Wilson. It would be best for him to avoid all contact with that woman.

Instead, Sage tried to make sense of the notes Ambrose had

handed off to him before disappearing. The papers were worn and creased in multiple spots, which made Sage wonder how long Ambrose had been carrying them around in his pocket. He ignored the stains on them and focused on the content.

The first page was just a summary of what was known so far about the case. Most of it was stuff Sage remembered from the original Unknown Suitor discussion on the forums. But the other pages contained new information. The four web sleuths had met up and driven to the spot where the body was found in the burned-out car. Sage was surprised to learn that the area wasn't nearly as remote as he had assumed it was. On one end, the place was only accessible down a long dirt driveway. From the other side, it was not far at all from the dumpster behind a twenty-four-hour pancake restaurant. According to Ambrose's notes, the dumpster could clearly be seen from where the car was found.

It felt like a new possible lead to Sage, but of course the police would have been aware of the proximity to the restaurant and would have interviewed all the staff back when the murder first occurred. After all these years, there wouldn't be any new information to uncover there.

A picture had been taken of the ring and shared with some different experts. It was a simple, plain style, which didn't help much with identification, but more than one expert believed it matched a ring that had been sold in Kmart stores more than two decades ago. That didn't really help to narrow things down, but it did mean if the Unknown Suitor had purchased the ring, he would likely have done so at some sort of secondhand place like a thrift shop. Sage thought this just lent credence to his belief that the ring had been stolen.

Sage didn't see anything in the notes about whether or not a DNA test had ever been performed, but he did see something very interesting on the last page of Ambrose's notes. It was a handwritten notation that read simply: Atkins PD. It could have meant anything, but Sage had a hunch he knew what it was.

end coffee shop was quintessential Atkins in Sage's opinion, and as he watched an endless stream of women in designer clothes coming in for their espresso fix, he was reminded of his old hometown. Atkins was probably a little more posh than Pleasant Oaks, but certainly the residents of Atkins would have got along swimmingly with the Pleasant Oaks Country Club set.

He had explained to Giselle that he was working with Penny on the online investigation, but she had stopped answering her emails, and he was concerned.

"The police really don't seem to be taking Penny's disappearance seriously," Giselle said. "They think she went away on vacation and just didn't bother to tell anyone or something, but she's not like that, and she wouldn't have just abandoned her birds."

"But you don't know what happened to her?" Sage asked.

"A couple of years ago, she dated this guy who turned into one of those crazy ex types," Giselle said. "So I thought maybe it had something to do with him, but the police say it's not him. I just don't know if I can believe them. They seem so incompetent."

"But you work for the police," Sage pointed out.

"Yeah, but I'm not a cop," she said. "All I'm saying is they're lucky no real crimes ever happen in Atkins, because they would never get solved with those dingleberries working the case."

Sage felt a knot forming in his stomach. As far as he knew, there never had been a serious crime in Atkins, but the same could not be said for Pleasant Oaks, and six years later the dingleberries of the Pleasant Oaks police force still hadn't managed to catch Melodie's killer.

"Well, I guess that will all change now that they have their rapid DNA testing machine," Sage said.

14

ATKINS, Pennsylvania, was only a couple of zip codes away from Culver Creek, but the affluent town full of large, well-maintained houses and luxury cars was a world away from Culver Creek in some ways. While Culver Creek's police struggled to make do with a budget that wasn't quite big enough, the Atkins police department had money to burn on things like rapid DNA testing machines, something Sage knew from the memo he had read from the county state police before he was let go from the Culver Creek police department.

Giselle Rosings fixed Sage with a suspicious stare, and Sage wondered if she could see right through his story. He had dug through his old emails to get her name, and reached her by calling the main number for the Atkins police department. Giselle was the tech who worked the rapid DNA testing machine that the Atkins PD had recently acquired. She also turned out to be a friend of Penny, aka CockatielOwner56.

That was the only reason she had agreed to meet with Sage at an espresso bar and gluten-free bakery in Atkins. The high-

"Yeah, well, the machine's only as good as what gets fed into it," Giselle said. "You can't identify a criminal with DNA if you don't take a sample and analyze it. Like that whole Unknown Suitor thing your crew and Penny were working on."

"What do you mean?" Sage already regretted the lies he had told her. Clearly, he was in the dark, and he was pretty sure Giselle could see the confusion written on his face.

"Well, I mean that guy got himself killed like six years ago, right? And it's not until a bunch of amateurs start messing around with testing DNA that they realize he was related to someone else who was murdered that same year."

"You found out his identity?" Sage was so eager, he nearly shouted the question at her. She gave him another suspicious look.

"Didn't your brother Phil tell you all this?" Giselle asked.

"My brother Phil?"

"Oh, right, that's his username. That's what Penny was always calling him."

Sage realized she meant PhillyFury.

"Oh, you mean Ambrose." He tried to remember all the lies he had told Giselle over the phone. He didn't remember saying anything about Ambrose being his brother, but perhaps he had? Maybe she had just misunderstood him. Either way, he knew better than to correct her now.

"Right, Ambrose," Giselle said. "He didn't tell you about the other murder victim?"

He most certainly had not, and now Sage felt his senses tingling. There had been nothing about it in the notes Ambrose gave him. It did seem like a key piece of information.

"The thing is, because this guy, your unknown suitor, was murdered in Maryland and the other victim was here in Pennsylvania, somehow no one picked up on it. That's what I mean about police incompetence."

"But the identity of the Unknown Suitor?" Sage asked.

"Okay, yeah, that still hasn't been figured out, but the way I look at it is, you start with the other murder victim—well, her family at least. One of them has to know something about this Unknown Suitor. They're pretty closely related, probably half siblings."

"And what was the name of the other murder victim?" Sage's heart was racing. He felt feverishly hot.

"Your brother said he knew the case," Giselle said. "That there was a forum thread about it."

"Oh, oh right," Sage said. "That case." Sweat began to pour off him. He was pretty sure his face looked like an oil slick.

"There's something else," Giselle said. "There's another relative. Probably another half sibling. It only showed up in the state database the other day, but it looks like it's from an old case. Probably some police department finally getting around to digitizing their records. But it's maybe another possible lead for finding out the identity of your John Doe, and this one isn't a murder victim."

Giselle pulled a piece of paper out of her handbag, unfolded it, and handed it to Sage. His sweat-damp fingers left a mark on the crisp, white paper. He glanced down at it and saw it was a printout that said "relative finder."

The name John Doe was followed by two all-too-familiar names. Melodie Dorian was the name that jumped out at him first. But before the shock had a chance to fully register, he saw the other name printed there—Zoey Wilson.

"You look like you've seen a ghost," Giselle said.

You're related, was what Zoey told him Melodie's ghost had said. What if the "you're" in this case wasn't Melodie and Sage, but Zoey and Sage. Wouldn't it make more sense if Melodie was talking to Zoey?

Ghosts didn't exist, but neither did one-in-a-million chances like this.

It wasn't until several minutes later, when Sage, in a state of shock, was driving home from his meeting with Giselle, that he realized something else. He wasn't an only child. He had half siblings out there. Well, at least one who was still alive.

15

SAGE FINALLY DID the thing he had been putting off for too long. He called his mother. He got a taste of his own medicine. Her voicemail picked up, and he left a stammering, meandering message that he immediately regretted. Well, it had been two weeks since he last talked to her, and he had a lot to say. Mostly what he had were questions.

One of those questions was *What is Zoey Wilson's cell phone number?* but who knew how long it would be before his mother decided to return his call. He knew all too well how his mother meted out justice, and he figured it was unlikely she would bother to return his call for twenty-four hours, at least.

Zoey Wilson's new website was under construction. That was what the little animated graphic said. Sage had seen her old website that had a heavy occult influence. That wouldn't have worked for Zoey's new and improved image. A Google search brought up one of Zoey's old listings, but when he called the cell number there, he got an out-of-service message. Apparently her reinvention had also included a brand-new phone number. There was an office number. He hesitated. He didn't feel comfortable calling Zoey's office line.

Memories of the other afternoon flashed through his head, and the heat rose in his face. He had acted inappropriately, and now he realized with a mixture of horror and revulsion that he had kissed his half sister.

He needed to talk to her. He picked his phone back up, ready to call her office line, when another thought came to him. He knew where she lived. Was it borderline obsessive for him to show up at her apartment? Instead of answering the question, he grabbed his jacket and keys and headed out the door.

H er father answered the door to Zoey's apartment. The man had only recently been released from prison, after being falsely convicted for murdering one of his former music students. Sage had a nagging thought about Victor Wilson and his false conviction, but staring at the man, it was drowned out by a much more pressing and overwhelming thought.

Looking into Victor Wilson's face, it was clear that he and Zoey were related. They shared so many similarities in their features. And if Zoey and Victor were father and daughter, then that must mean Victor was his father as well, but Sage struggled to see any of himself in Victor's face. Victor was a big bear of a man, and so in terms of size, if nothing else, Sage could pass for Victor's son. Hadn't people always remarked that Sage must have gotten his height and build from his mother's side of the family?

"Can I help you?" Victor asked.

"I was looking for Zoey," Sage said when he had recovered himself. He couldn't stop staring at Victor's face, looking for something familiar there.

"I remember you," Victor said. "You're that cop."

Victor didn't seem too pleased with this development. Sage couldn't say he blamed the guy. After all, it was cops, incompetent cops, who had gotten him sent away to prison.

"She's not here." Victor started to close the door.

Sage forced his foot into the doorjamb to stop it from shutting.

"Wait!" Sage said. "I need to talk to her about something. Do you have her cell phone number?"

"If she wanted you to have her number, I'm sure she would have given it to you."

Victor didn't shove him, exactly, just strongly forced Sage's foot out of the doorway.

"Do you have any children with another woman?" Sage shouted, and the door slammed in his face. That or his inappropriate question attracted the attention of one of Zoey's neighbors, an older woman who stared at Sage and gave him a wide berth as she walked past.

Sage was back in his car and still parked outside Zoey's building when a call came in from an unknown number. He swiped to answer, hoping, even though it was unlikely Victor had called his daughter and told her Sage had shown up.

His heart leapt when he heard her voice, and he didn't even let her finish her greeting.

"I need to talk to you," he said. The words tumbled out of his mouth. "I'm sorry about showing up at your apartment. I shouldn't have done that, but I didn't know how else to get ahold of you, and—"

"Sage!" She shouted his name because just saying it in a normal tone hadn't been enough to get him to shut up.

"It's your mother," she said. "She was taken to the hospital."

16

JUSTIN WAS STILL shaky as he drove home from work. He started to head back toward his apartment, but some sort of instinct took over, and he found himself getting on the highway and driving back toward Pleasant Oaks. Had he been able to hear the voice of reason over the voices in his head, he might have second-guessed this decision, but as it was, he felt powerless to do anything but drive guided by instinct.

Of course, he knew where Melodie had lived. After her murder, pictures of the home had been splashed across the television news and printed in the local newspapers. In the aftermath of the murder, the street had been crowded with news crews and gawkers. Justin had once been one of those gawkers.

He didn't remember the exact address, but it turned out instincts or some sort of muscle memory had no problem guiding him straight there. He recognized the road as soon as he turned down it. Staying below the twenty-five miles per hour posted speed limit was no problem as he rolled slowly down the road. He glided to a stop in front of Melodie's house. There was a for-sale sign posted in the front lawn.

This was where Melodie had grown up. That was what they said on the news. Justin imagined her as a cute little girl posing for first-day-of-school pictures in front of the house, learning to ride a bike in the driveway. As he stared at the perfect-looking house and the perfect-looking yard, he could almost see a miniature version of Melodie running around and laughing. It filled him with joy to think of her this way.

He was so busy watching an imaginary little girl playing in the front yard, he didn't at first notice that in real life the front door had opened and woman was peering out. Was it Kelly, Melodie's mother? He didn't know if she still lived here, but if it was her, he could get out of the car and go apologize to her.

The idea of stepping outside the safety of his vehicle frightened him, and he was reminded of another time he couldn't work up the courage to get out of his car, a night long ago.

By the time he got to the hospital, it was too late.

"It was over very quickly," the nurse said. "She was unconscious when the paramedics brought her in, and the internal injuries were too severe."

The nurse handed him a clear plastic bag.

"Her effects," the nurse explained.

Justin's mind, in a state of shock, played the word *effects* on an endless loop as he puzzled over what a strange word it was. He stared at the contents of the plastic bag: his mother's wallet, her keyring, the cheap wedding ring she always wore.

How was it that a person's entire life could be reduced to this—some random items in a plastic bag?

"Did she say anything?" Justin asked. His mother wasn't the sort of person to go on walks, and she certainly never walked anywhere at night. When he left the house, she had already changed into her pajamas, and she was watching television. He fully expected her to still be planted there on the couch when he returned, no doubt snoring away.

Why tonight of all nights had she been walking somewhere, especially after what he told her?

The nurse shook her head. "No, sweetie, she was unconscious. I'm sorry."

"It's okay," Justin said, even though nothing at all was okay. He should have been there. This was all his fault. He never went anywhere. He was always home. Why had he needed to go out tonight?

"Do you have someone to stay with?" the nurse asked.

It was his turn to shake his head. He had no one, no one at all. His whole life, it had been just the two of them, him and his mother.

Sirens rang out as an ambulance approached, and the emergency staff mobilized and started to race toward the door.

"Here, this might help," the nurse said, and she thrust a pamphlet at him. "I'm sorry, I have to go."

He watched her rush over to meet the incoming ambulance with the rest of the staff members before glancing down at the pamphlet. "Mourning the Loss of a Loved One: Resources for the Bereaved" it read in light blue letters. He carried it and the plastic bag of belongings back to the car.

The tears came as soon as he sat down behind the steering wheel. Once the waterworks had been switched on, there was no stopping the flood. For the second time that night, he realized he was making a scene in a public parking lot, but this time he didn't care.

When the tears finally slowed down to a trickle, he swiped at his puffy eyes and started up the car. In a dazed state, he drove home to an empty, silent house.

The police showed up two days later.

17

SAGE KNEW his pacing was making the other people waiting in the hospital's emergency room nervous, but he didn't care. Let them be nervous. He certainly was. It had been fifteen minutes since he arrived. Although the staff had confirmed that his mother had been brought in, they refused to give him any kind of update.

He went up to the reception window again, and this time the woman behind it didn't even try to mask her annoyance.

"Look, I told you someone would let you know as soon as there was more information. Now, please have a seat."

"I just need to know if she's going to be okay," Sage said.

"As I explained, someone will let you know as soon as we have more information."

He was reminded of a night six years ago. Instead of a hospital emergency room, he had been pacing around the living room because there was no emergency room on earth that could save his sister. Then, they had been waiting for the phone to ring or the police to return to the house and give them the news they longed to hear: they had found and arrested

Melodie's murderer. But six years later they were still waiting to hear that news. Sometimes Sage felt like he had spent six years pacing around the living room. That might as well have been what he was doing these past six years for all the good it did his sister.

"Sage!"

He turned at the shout and saw his father run in through the automatic doors.

"What's going on?" his father shouted. "I got your text."

"I don't know," Sage said. "Nobody will tell me anything." He looked pointedly at the woman behind the window, but she ignored him.

According to Zoey, she had been scheduled to meet his mom at the house. She got nervous when his mom wasn't answering the door, then she saw the broken kitchen window. So she used the lockbox to get into the house and found his mom sprawled out on the kitchen floor in a pool of blood. There was a brick on the floor beside her.

"Just like the other day," Zoey said.

Sage had relayed all this to his father over the phone as he drove to the hospital, but since he arrived he hadn't been told anything, nor been allowed to see his mother.

Sage looked up and saw a gray-haired man in a lab coat in the doorway of the emergency room. Everything about the man screamed doctor. Sage jumped to his feet before the man even said his name.

He led Sage and his father into a hallway off the emergency room.

"Is she okay?" Sage asked.

"She's stable," the doctor said.

"Stable?"

"Your mother sustained a head injury. She lost a lot of blood. I'm afraid at the moment she is in a coma."

"Oh God," his father said. His face looked gray as he leaned against the wall for support.

"Can we see her?" Sage asked.

"Of course," the doctor said.

Sage wasn't prepared for seeing his strong, capable mother looking so helpless in the hospital bed. His father ran to her side. He smoothed the hair back from her forehead as tears rolled down his face, but Sage couldn't force himself to take more than a step inside the room.

He couldn't help feeling like this was somehow his fault. It had been two weeks since he had spoken to his mother. There was no reason to think that speaking to her could have saved her from this, but if he'd been speaking to her, he would have told her about the other brick—the one that almost hit Zoey.

Maybe with that warning, she would have been a little more careful, maybe avoided standing in front of windows when speeding cars were headed up the street. He thought of something else, the note attached to the last brick that had been thrown. What if that brick and this one had both been intended to hit his mother? Did this brick have a note too, and what did it say?

"There's something I have to do," Sage said. His father looked up.

"Wait," his dad said. "There's something we need to talk about."

Now his father finally wanted to have the conversation they should have had years ago? Unbelievable. Sage gave a rueful little shake of his head.

"I'll be back," Sage said.

~

"How is she?"

Sage had a million thoughts racing through his head as he walked across the hospital parking lot, and it took a moment or two for him to realize the shouted question was meant for him. Zoey ran toward him from the other side of the lot.

"The police finally let me go," she said. "I told them about the other day, and they had all these questions."

"She's in a coma," Sage said.

Zoey gasped.

"It was supposed to be me," she said.

"I don't know about that," Sage said.

"No," Zoey insisted. "It was. Think about it. The other day? That brick was thrown right at me. And today? I was supposed to be there, but I was running late. If I had been on time, this never would have happened."

"You don't know that," Sage said. He thought of the note on the brick. *Murderer.* Did someone think Zoey and not her sister was the one who murdered Zoey's boyfriend and, all those years ago, her father's music student? There was a nagging thought again at the back of his head, but this time Sage thought he knew exactly what it was about, what he had learned when he met with Giselle.

Did his mother already know Zoey was his half sister? Was that why she hired Zoey to sell her house?

"Did my mother say anything to you about—"

"She was unconscious when I got there," Zoey said, but Sage had been thinking about before. Instead of clarifying, he asked another question.

"What about the brick that hit her?" Sage asked. "Was there a note on it?"

Zoey shook her head, but then she said, "I don't know. I was so worried about your mom. I called 9-1-1 and then I was trying to do something to stop the bleeding. Her head was bleeding so much."

Zoey began to cry, and Sage laid a comforting hand on her shoulder, but he felt an almost electric jolt of heat, and what had happened the other afternoon flashed through his head. He removed his hand quickly.

"It's not your fault," he assured her. "Do you know if the police took the brick as evidence?"

"They must have, right?" she said.

He nodded his agreement, but inside he was doubting the basic competency of the Pleasant Oaks Police Department.

"I should go talk to them," he said.

He had, in fact, talked to members of the Pleasant Oaks Police Department on numerous occasions, something that now seemed to be a bit of an inconvenience. Talked, maybe, was a generous way to describe some of the tirades he had gone on while in the police station. As far as he knew, he wasn't specifically forbidden from setting foot inside the Pleasant Oaks PD, but he was definitely persona non grata around there.

"They were asking if there was any security camera footage," Zoey said. "I didn't know if your mom has any cameras up."

"Not that I'm aware of," Sage said, but what did she need cameras for when she had nosy old Mr. Felton across the street? "There's someone I need to talk to."

18

JUSTIN WAS surprised when he heard a knock on his apartment door early Saturday morning. He peered through a little window and saw the patch on the navy-blue sleeve of the police officer's uniform.

He opened the door without removing the chain.

"Virgil Chandler?" the officer asked. Justin nodded. "Mind if I come in for a chat?"

Justin removed the chain, then opened the door for the police officer to step inside. The cop scrutinized the apartment. It was a small space, but Justin kept it tidy. His decorating style was pretty spare and simple.

"Your neighbors suggested I talk to you," the cop said. He was holding a brick wrapped in a plastic bag in his hand. "Multiple neighbors," the cop added with more drama than Justin cared for. "So I looked into you, and turns out you have quite the rap sheet. I also saw you just got out of a stint in the state mental hospital."

Justin shrugged.

"Well, I'll get right to the point," the cop said. "Do you recognize this?" He held up the brick in the plastic bag.

"It's a brick," Justin said.

"Yeah, that's right, Einstein. It's a brick." The cop narrowed his eyes at Justin like he was trying to stare straight into his soul.

Brick dick, the voices in his head said. Justin ignored them. *He has a kid he doesn't know about. Little pisser doesn't know his brick dick daddy. Sound familiar?*

Justin shook his head to clear the chatter.

"What are you shaking your head for?" the cop growled. "I didn't ask you a question."

"Ear infection," Justin said.

"Nutjob," the cop muttered. "You know where I found this brick? I bet you do, Einstein." Justin hesitated about shaking his head again, so the cop continued. "Found it on the backseat of your neighbor's car along with all the glass from their smashed back window. You have any idea how it might have gotten there?"

"Someone threw it?" Justin asked. The voices in his head seemed really taken with the phrase "brick dick" and kept repeating it.

"Ooh, you're regular old detective material, ain't you?"

Justin almost made the mistake of shaking his head again.

"What I think is that you threw it there, Virgil."

"I didn't," Justin blurted out.

The cop walked over to the wall where Justin's bookshelf was, and Justin realized what he was looking at. His bookshelf was really just some wood boards propped up with stacks of red bricks. Bricks that looked remarkably similar to the one in the cop's hand.

"It would be crooked," Justin said.

"What's that?" the cop asked.

Justin walked over to the shelf beside the police officer.

"The shelf would be crooked if any of the bricks were missing."

"Shelf seems kind of short to me," the cop said. "I mean, you're a tall guy, right? What are you, six two, six three?"

"Six three," Justin said.

"Right? So why is this shelf so short?"

"That's all the books I have," Justin said. He didn't like this cop in his space studying his stuff. He fully expected the officer to start making some snide remarks about the titles on the shelf, most of which were about psychic gifts and channeling messages from other realms, but the cop must have been illiterate.

"What I think is there used to be another shelf here," the cop said. "But you had to take it down because you threw one of the bricks through your neighbor's car window."

"I didn't," Justin said.

"Well, I've got my eye on you, crazy man."

Brick dick. Brick dick. Brick dick.

At first, Justin had gotten nervous when the police cruiser pulled into the parking lot. He was an orphan now, and he was worried they were going to take him away and put him in foster care. Then he reminded himself that he turned eighteen a few weeks ago. He was legally an adult. It didn't matter that he felt like a little boy who desperately missed his mommy.

As he watched the police officer walking slowly toward the building and trying to decide whether he should go to the front door where a CLOSED sign was prominently displayed in the window or go around to the back door, Justin realized the police officer was probably here to give him some sort of report on his mother's death. So Justin unlocked the front door and stuck his head out to call out a friendly hello.

The officer picked up his pace and now walked confidently up the front walk.

"Are you Justin Turner?" the police officer asked. Justin nodded. "I'm Officer Walt Briggs. May I come in?"

The psychic storefront wasn't exactly conducive to entertaining or, in this case, having a conversation with a police officer, but Justin made the most of it.

"Do you have a photo ID?" Officer Briggs asked.

Justin went and retrieved his driver's license. The police officer handed it back to him after scrutinizing it.

"We had someone in custody the other night with a driver's license with your name and address on it." Briggs showed Justin a computer printout of a photo. "Do you recognize this man?"

Justin shook his head, but he was finally making sense of what the police officer had said.

"The other night," Justin said. "Is that why my mother was walking toward town?"

"A phone call was made to this number," Briggs said. "We asked if there was a Justin Turner who resided here and explained that he was in custody."

"Oh," Justin said. His knees felt too weak to support him. He sat down in the chair the clients normally used. The only reason his mother had left the house was because she thought he was at the police station. She was on her way to rescue him. He shook his head. "Wait, why did that guy have a driver's license with my name and address on it?"

"We think you might be a victim of identity theft," Briggs said. "It's our understanding that the individual in question has used multiple identities."

"Is he still there?" Justin said. "I want to talk to him."

"Unfortunately, we were forced to release him, but we

wanted to make sure you were aware of the situation, and let you know that it would be in your best interest to sign up for a credit monitoring service."

Walt Briggs was starting to make his way toward the door.

"But what about that guy?" Justin asked. "Don't you know anything about him?"

Justin half wondered if the guy was even real. What if he was some sort of ghost? Not a ghost exactly, but like the voices he heard taking on a physical manifestation so they could exact their revenge on Justin for failing to deliver their warning. Once the job was done, this so-called man who claimed to be Justin had vanished into thin air.

"I'm sorry," Briggs said. "I don't know what to tell you. We kind of have our hands full right now. You heard about that girl who was murdered?"

Oh, Justin had heard all about it. "Long before you did," he muttered.

"What's that?" The officer frowned at Justin.

Justin just shook his head. "Nothing."

"Look, I think that guy's real name is Virgil Chandler," Officer Briggs said. "But listen, kid, don't do anything stupid, okay?"

19

MR. FELTON DIDN'T HAVE security cameras because he didn't believe in "all them doodads."

"Yeah, I saw a suspicious car around that time," Mr. Felton said.

They stood on Mr. Felton's front stoop, which had an unobstructed view of the Dorian home across the way.

"My mom's real estate agent was here," Sage explained. "You sure it wasn't her car you saw?"

"Does your mom's real estate agent drive a beat-up old station wagon?"

"No, nothing like that," Sage said.

"Well, I guess it wasn't the real estate agent then," Mr. Felton said. "I wrote down the license plate number, if you want that."

"Yes, definitely!" Sage couldn't believe the old man hadn't led with that information.

~

Sage sat huddled over his cup of green tea at the table in the back of the coffee shop, watching the door. He perked up when Rod finally walked in.

"We've got to stop meeting like this," Rod said as he sat down across from Sage. He was trying for a jocular tone, but Sage could detect an undercurrent of seriousness.

"You want a coffee or something?" Sage asked.

"I want to know what the hell is going on," Rod said. "Is everything okay?"

It was a loaded question, and Sage wasn't sure how to answer it. His text to Rod had insisted it was urgent and that Rod should meet him here ASAP.

"I need you to run a tag number for me," Sage said.

"You could have come into the station for this," Rod said.

"I feel like I'm not especially well-liked over there. With everything that happened, I didn't think my presence would be welcome."

"What happened is you got canned unfairly," Rod said. "No one's going to hold that against you."

"And the whole country club thing?" Sage said.

"Come on, who among us hasn't sneaked our way into a country club to harass a senator."

"Senator's son," Sage muttered.

"Look, believe me when I say no one cares about that whole mess," Rod said. "But I'm gonna be blunt here. Since you got sacked, you've been acting pretty damn weird."

"I've got a lot going on," Sage said. "I've found out something about my sister—well, a possible connection to another murder."

Rod held up the note with the tag number written on it that Sage had handed him.

"This have something to do with that?" he asked.

"Maybe," Sage said. "I don't know. Someone threw a rock through my mother's window. Hit her in the head. She's in the hospital. In a coma."

"What?" Rod's voice was so loud that everyone in the coffee shop turned to stare. "I mean, why the hell didn't you say something?"

"I just did," Sage said.

Rod shook his head like his former coworker was absolutely out of his mind.

"Can I ask a question?" Rod said. Sage shrugged. "Why am I looking up this number? Why didn't you bring this to the police investigating what happened to your mom?"

"Let's just say I'm not exactly a welcome presence in that police station."

"You better watch out, you keep up this habit of making friends and influencing people and you won't be able to set foot in a single police department in the state."

"Yeah, well, and I don't trust those nitwits not to bungle this like they've bungled everything else."

20

BEFORE JUSTIN HAD a chance to sit down at his workstation, Lennie waved him into his office. Justin had been afraid of this. He hadn't been in since leaving abruptly four days ago. He called in sick the following day, then had two days off, and naively he hoped maybe the whole thing would blow over. Clearly this had not occurred.

"Here's the thing," Lennie said. "You're good. You're one of my top earners, but you're like a . . ." Lennie waved his hand in the air like he was searching for the perfect word. "A wild cannon," he finally finished. "You understand what I'm saying?"

Justin did. He was pretty sure his boss meant loose cannon, and he nodded to show his understanding.

"That frightens me," Lennie said. "I run a tight ship, and wild cannons are dangerous things."

Loose cannon, loose cannon, the voices repeated in his head. Justin was just thankful they weren't saying brick dick, which seemed to be their new favorite mantra.

"I'm sorry," Justin mumbled, ignoring the chatter in his head.

"We need to talk about what happened the other day." Lennie steepled his fingers and looked thoughtfully at some random spot on the wall. "Let me ask you a question. Are you close with your mother?"

"She passed away," Justin said.

"I suspected as much, Virgil," Lennie said. "You know, when I heard how emotional you got while talking to that customer about the son who wasn't returning her calls, I thought to myself, here's a young man who has some issues with his own mother."

Justin blinked in surprise. He hadn't expected this turn of events, and he was a bit annoyed that the voices couldn't have been useful for once and given him a heads-up.

"Look, the thing is," Lennie continued, "difficult as it may be, when we're talking to a customer, we have to try not to let our own personal lives enter the conversation. Are we clear on that?"

Justin gave another nod of understanding. He was a bit stunned. It seemed like he wasn't going to get fired after all.

"Did you have any questions?"

"What happens if someone calls up that we know?" Justin asked. He blurted the words out without even thinking, and hated himself for sabotaging himself like that. He had been a few seconds away from putting this whole ugly blunder behind him, but now he had to go and mess everything up.

"Well, the likelihood of that happening is pretty slim," his boss said. Then he seemed to reconsider his words, because he said, "Wait, has that happened? Was that woman you hung up on someone you knew?"

Justin prayed that Lennie didn't go back and review the transcript, because if he did, he would very clearly see that

Justin's distress had only begun once the caller told him her name.

"No, nothing like that," Justin said quickly. "I was just thinking that it might happen sometime."

"Well, if it does happen, you can always have someone else jump on the call," Lennie suggested.

"Okay, thank you," Justin said, relieved that his stupid blurted-out comment hadn't ruined everything.

"I'm glad we had this conversation." Lennie stood up, indicating that his lecture had reached its conclusion. "And remember, if you have any questions at all, or anything you want to talk about, my door is always open."

Although skinny, balding Lennie with his bad skin and out-of-style glasses looked nothing like Walt Briggs, Justin was reminded of the kind-hearted police officer he had known all those years ago, and he felt that gnawing empty place in his heart as he thought of one more person who had been lost to him.

Justin knew that Officer Walt Briggs was taking pity on him. That was why he had shown up a few times after his initial visit, always bringing something with him—a tray of food his wife had made or a bag of fast food. He asked if Justin was keeping up with schoolwork, and if there was anything he needed help with. None of this was part of his official duties. Justin wasn't a ward of the state, but Briggs was a nice guy.

"So have you thought about what your plans are, long term?" Briggs asked one afternoon as the two of them ate greasy fast-food hamburgers in Justin's kitchen.

The week before, Briggs had surprised Justin by showing

up for his high school graduation. So Justin understood where this talk about planning for the future was coming from.

"I don't know," Justin said. "I got a job at the country club. So I guess I'll do that for now."

"Well, that's fine for a summer job," Briggs said, "but you should give some thought to what you would like to do with your life."

This was something Justin had given some thought to. He had heard what the voices had to say on this subject, but he wasn't much interested in their opinion.

"How would I get a job like yours?" Justin asked.

"A cop?" Briggs asked, surprised, but Justin noticed the way his mentor's eyes lit up. "Well, there's an exam you would have to take, but here's the thing, if you go to school, even community college, and study criminal justice, it will give you a leg up, and maybe even help you to get a detective job down the road."

"Do you think that's something I could do?" Justin asked.

"Of course!" Briggs made no attempt to hide his excitement. "I could help you with your studies, too. Give you some pointers."

"Thanks," Justin said. He grabbed another french fry.

Briggs started talking about what being a cop was like, and why Justin would like it. He talked a mile a minute, and Justin could barely keep up with it all. So Justin didn't get a chance to ask him about the other thing—all the notices he kept getting from the mortgage company. It was just as well. There was nothing Officer Walt Briggs was going to be able to do about that.

Justin tried to focus on this advice his friend and mentor was giving him, even as the voices in his head told him he was wasting his time, that he was never going to become a cop.

21

SAGE AWOKE to what sounded like a jackhammer. He jerked his head up too quickly and pulled a muscle in his neck. Well, that was what he got for sleeping on the couch. Because apparently he had fallen asleep on the couch once again. The jackhammer was still going, but now he realized it wasn't a jackhammer at all but someone knocking on his door, someone very persistently knocking on his door.

As he shuffled toward it, he glanced at the clock on the microwave and saw it was 1:15. He wasn't sure if that was a.m. or p.m. until he noticed the sun streaming through the window. Just as he slid the chain off the door, it occurred to him that he probably should have at least glanced in a mirror before greeting his persistent guest, but it was too late for that now.

He opened the door, figuring it had to be Rod with the information on that plate number, but he had figured wrong. Zoey Wilson stood in the hallway, her fist raised, poised to continue pounding the suddenly open door. Her expression was murderous. He really, really regretted not taking a pass by the mirror before going to the door. He knew he looked like hell on earth.

Zoey pushed right past him and into his apartment like she owned the place. It took him a moment to get over being stunned and remember to shut the door.

"Come in," he said sarcastically. "Have a seat. Can I get you anything? Something to drink? A snack?"

She didn't sit down and ignored his offer of a drink or a snack, and instead launched into a full-on snarling attack.

"Where the hell do you get the nerve?" she demanded.

"I don't know what—"

"You show up at my apartment, start harassing my dad, who for the record has not been treated especially fairly by people in your profession, then give him the impression that I'm some sort of criminal who is in trouble with the law."

"I never said—"

"I'm not done!" she screamed at him. "I don't know what kind of weirdo you are, but I've dated psychos before, and I really don't need any more psychos in my life right now. So you leave my father alone, and you need to stop stalking me."

"You know what," he said. "I think I'm going to help myself to a drink. You sure I can't get you anything?"

He went past her into the kitchen, grabbed one of only two clean glasses left in his cabinet, and then stared at it. Six years. That was how long it had been since he took a sip of alcohol, but as he took the glass out, he was picturing pouring himself a drink of something strong. Strange, since he didn't keep so much as a can of beer in his refrigerator. He shook off the weird feeling, and instead pulled a gallon jug of spring water from his fridge.

"Some water?" he called out to Zoey.

"Yeah, okay, sure, I'll have a glass of water."

A few seconds later, he returned to the living room carrying two glasses of water. She had finally taken a seat on his lumpy couch. He handed off one of the glasses to her and took a seat in the chair opposite her without bothering to remove the papers he had piled up there.

"How's your mother?" she asked in a remarkably calmer tone after she had taken a sip of water.

"About the same," he said. She nodded.

"She know about you getting fired?" Zoey asked. He raised an eyebrow. "I showed up at the police station looking for you," she said by way of explanation.

"Ah," he said. "I suppose that went well."

"Your friend Rod gave me your address," Zoey explained.

"Some friend," Sage said. "I can't believe he didn't text me a warning."

"He tried to call you, but he said your phone must be off because it went straight to voicemail."

Sage glanced at the coffee table, where his phone was sitting. He tried to remember the last time he charged it. He picked it up, but the phone was completely dead. So he grabbed the charger and plugged it into the wall.

"I figure it's some sort of criminal offense to show up at someone's door impersonating a police officer," Zoey said. "Harassing an old man."

"I wasn't harassing anyone," Sage said, "and I wasn't impersonating a police officer."

"No? Then what the hell were you doing?"

"There's something I need to talk to you about," he said.

She stood up from the couch, downed the rest of her glass of water in one big and impressive gulp, and carried the empty glass into the kitchen. So that meant not only had she seen him with his serious bedhead and rumpled clothes, but she had also got a glimpse of his kitchen sink overflowing with unwashed dishes.

"If this is about what happened the other day," she said from the kitchen, "on your mother's front lawn, then you should know I've already put that out of my mind."

"Clearly," he muttered.

She came out of the kitchen and gave him a pointed look.

"I have to go," she said.

"Sit down," he said. "You just got here."

She made her way back to the door.

"Sit down," he said again.

"I don't need any more psychos in my life," she said.

"Well, unfortunately you're related to one."

That got her attention. She turned around and stood leering down at him.

"For your information, my father is not some psycho," she said. "He's a hero, that's what he is, and you have no right to talk trash about him like that, considering the way you live." She waved an arm around to indicate his disaster of an apartment, and though she was too kind to say it, he suspected she was thinking of his appearance as well.

"I wasn't talking about your father," he said. "I meant me."

"What?"

"We're half siblings," he said.

She looked at him like he had really lost it. This wasn't the way he had imagined telling her, but she hadn't left him much choice.

"I don't understand," she said.

"Remember how you said you saw my sister's ghost? And she said 'You're related'? I think that's what she meant. You're my half sister."

"I'd lost a lot of blood at that point," Zoey said. "I'm pretty sure I was hallucinating."

"Well, regardless, we're half siblings."

"But I don't understand how that could be," Zoey said.

"Unfortunately the one woman who could tell us is in a coma right now."

"Not the only woman who could tell us," Zoey said quietly.

His phone suddenly had enough juice to power up, and it came alive with an overwhelming amount of alerts. He grabbed the phone and scrolled through, seeing two missed calls from Rod from about a half hour ago, and then a little before that, a text from Rod. It was a name and address for someone named Virgil Chandler. Looked like Rod had a chance to run that plate number.

"So how did you—" Zoey began, but Sage stood up before she could finish speaking.

"Sorry," he said. "I need to go."

He grabbed his jacket from where he had left it slung over a chair.

"You might want to grab some pants," Zoey said.

"What?" He looked down and saw to his dismay that he was wearing only a pair of boxer shorts. "Oh God. I'm sorry."

She shrugged. "It's cool. We're family, right?"

22

MAYBE IT WAS proof they were related that only a short while after Zoey had shown up at his place pounding on his door like she was ready to pound her fist right through it, he was performing the same abuse on another apartment door. This particular one belonged to one Virgil Chandler. Either Virgil was more cautious about opening his door than Sage was, or more likely, he wasn't home.

"What did that psycho do now?"

Sage turned around and saw one of Virgil's neighbors eyeing him.

"Do you know Virgil?" Sage asked. "Do you know where he is?"

The neighbor shrugged. "Maybe they hauled him off to the looney bin again. I heard he threw a brick through someone's window."

Sage felt dizzy. Maybe he had underestimated the Pleasant Oaks Police Department. It sounded like they must have already caught Virgil.

"Do you know if he was arrested?" Sage asked.

The neighbor shrugged again.

After failing to get anywhere on the phone—the woman on the dispatch desk had promised to relay his question to the officer in charge of the investigation, but he didn't have a whole lot of faith in that happening anytime soon—Sage decided to drive to Pleasant Oaks and get everything sorted out. He figured he could get to the bottom of things and still have time to get to the hospital for visiting hours.

He wondered if he was being too optimistic. It was true he hadn't gotten anywhere on the phone, but he knew from experience that showing up there in person was even more of a gamble. His past histrionics at the police station had earned him a certain reputation, and getting the time of day, let alone information on his mother's case, might prove to be something of an impossibility.

But he had another idea. If the investigation was ongoing, there might be an officer at the house or somewhere in the vicinity, talking to the neighbors, examining the shattered window. It was worth a shot, and it would hardly be out of line for Sage to show up at his mother's house.

As soon as he pulled down her street he saw that this was going to be nothing but a waste of time. There wasn't a cop car in sight, and judging by the fact that her taped-up kitchen window looked exactly the way it had when he last saw it, he was doubtful about how thorough a job the Pleasant Oaks Police Department was doing with the investigation. He pulled into her driveway and sat there idling as he debated whether or not he dared to show his face at the local police station. Visiting hours didn't start for more than an hour, so he had time. The worst thing they could do was throw him out of the station. It was a chance he was willing to take.

He popped the car into reverse and glanced in the rearview mirror as he rolled back down the driveway. Then he saw something that made him slam on his brakes. A battered old station wagon drove slowly down the road. Too slowly. Like someone was casing the place. Sage knew full well a psycho by the name of Virgil Chandler was behind the wheel.

He turned off his car, flung open the door, and ran after the old Subaru wagon. He slammed on the back hatch as soon as he caught up to the slow-moving vehicle.

"Hey!" he shouted. "Hey!"

The car braked and pulled over to the curb. Sage ran up to the driver's door. The driver rolled down his window. The car was so old it still had crank-style windows. Virgil Chandler sat there staring at him. He didn't look like a deranged psycho, but that was the thing with deranged psychos, they could look like average people.

Nervous energy coursed through Sage. He had no doubt he was staring at the man who put his mother in the hospital, but was he also staring at the man who murdered his sister?

"Get out of the car!" Sage roared.

"I was just—"

But Sage didn't give the man a chance to finish.

"Get out of the car!" Sage repeated, and he helped out by yanking open the door.

Virgil climbed out of the car. He held his hands up in a placating, I-don't-want-any-trouble sort of way. Sage was used to towering over people and was surprised to be looking right into Virgil's eyes.

"Were you here the other day?" Sage twitched with pent-up energy.

"I was just driving—"

"I said, were you here the other day?" Sage was getting tired of repeating himself.

Virgil nodded.

"You throw a brick through that window?" Sage demanded. He pointed at the taped-up kitchen window. Virgil followed his finger, then shook his head.

"No," he said.

"Don't lie to me!" Sage screamed. Behind him, he heard a door open. No doubt Mr. Felton was watching with his eagle eyes. "I know you threw a brick through that window. I want to know why."

"I didn't," Virgil stammered, and it almost sounded like he was going to cry, but Sage wasn't buying it. This guy was a stone-cold psycho, and Sage was sure this was all an act. "It's not what you think," Virgil said. "I knew her."

"You know my mother?" Sage asked.

"No, I knew the girl who used to live here, Melodie."

Sage lost all control. His fist sprang forth as if of its own volition. He hit Virgil Chandler square in the jaw, but he didn't stop there. Virgil tried to escape back into his car, but once his rage tap had been turned on, Sage felt unable to turn off the torrent of punches that pummeled the other man. There was something cathartic about the experience, and he had entered an altered state of mind as a meditative calm filled him even as he violently attacked his adversary.

Sage might never have stopped, but hands grabbed at him and pulled him away from Virgil. Sage blinked as he returned to reality and recognized Mr. Felton leaning over the injured man. Strong arms gripped Sage, but he pulled free and turned to see a man in a UPS uniform, his truck parked in a nearby driveway. Had the two men not intervened, he might still be beating that psycho.

"He's dangerous!" Sage warned them, pointing at where a bloody and battered Virgil had collapsed on the ground, but even he could see how ridiculous his statement was.

23

SAGE GLANCED at the clock as he collected his things from the officer on duty: a bloodstained jacket, his wallet, his cell phone with ten percent battery remaining. According to the clock, it was nearly eleven p.m. It had been a very long day.

The officer waiting to escort him from the premises was not the same one who had brought him in. This guy was older. His name tag read "BRIGGS." But Sage figured it didn't matter.

"You arrest that guy?" Sage asked.

"What? The guy you beat the living crap out of?" Briggs asked.

"Right, Virgil Chandler."

"Generally we don't arrest victims," Briggs said.

"My mother's in a coma because of him," Sage said.

"And his name's not Virgil."

"I think maybe there's a miscommunication here," Sage said. He was tired, but he still bristled with anger. Had these nitwit Pleasant Oaks cops let that bastard go? He couldn't help but feel like this whole thing was their way of getting revenge on him for his previous tirades against their ineptitude. "You're letting a criminal walk free."

"I know," Briggs said. "I can't believe they gave you bail, and someone actually paid it."

"Not me," Sage said. "That psycho Virgil."

"Only one psycho here," Briggs said. "And like I said, that guy's name ain't Virgil, it's Justin Turner."

Sage felt a chill pass through him. Had he beat up the wrong guy? He couldn't remember if he had checked the plate number on the guy's car. Could he have been that stupid? But he remembered something very clearly. The last thing Virgil—or Justin, if that was his name—had said before Sage landed his first punch: "I knew the girl who used to live here, Melodie."

R od was waiting for him in the parking lot of the Pleasant Oaks police station. He was standing beside his car. The expression on his face was unreadable in the orange glow of the parking lot's lights.

"Thanks," Sage said when he reached the car. "I owe you."

"You do, you definitely do," Rod said. "Come on, get in. Let's get out of here. The cops here are all giving me dirty looks."

"Yeah me and the Pleasant Oaks Police Department are like this," Sage said, holding his two fingers apart in a V shape.

Rod just shook his head and got behind the wheel of the car and started it up. Sage sat down in the passenger seat. His body felt impossibly tired, like if he crawled into a bed now, he could sleep for a week or more.

"What the hell is going on, man?" Rod asked as he pulled out onto the road.

Sage could have called his father to bail him out. Maybe he

should have, but Sage was ashamed. You shouldn't have to feel ashamed in front of your own family, but then as Sage had recently learned, his father wasn't really his family.

"You hear anything about that guy?" Sage asked.

"They took him to the hospital," Rod said, "but I think he's going to be fine, no thanks to you. What the hell were you thinking?"

"I wasn't," Sage admitted. Then he admitted something else. "I think I got the wrong guy."

"So who's the right guy?" Rod pulled up in front of Sage's mother's house. The old station wagon was long gone. Sage's car was still parked in the driveway.

"I don't know anymore," Sage said. "I thought he was Virgil Chandler, but the cop at the station just now said no."

"Virgil Chandler. That was the tag number you had me run," Rod said.

"Yeah," Sage said. "The brick-thrower, but I don't think that's who I beat up. But this guy said he knew Melodie."

"So, what, maybe an old boyfriend or something?" Rod asked.

Sage nodded as he mulled this over, but he knew that couldn't be true. Melodie's boyfriend had been Colin Hillman. Sage couldn't recall her ever mentioning someone named Justin Turner, but he could have been a friend from school. Only, why would a friend from school be skulking around the house six years after Melodie had been killed? Something didn't add up.

"You okay?" Rod asked.

Sage realized he had been sitting there silently for a minute or so while he tried to make sense of his muddled thoughts.

"Yeah," Sage said. "Just tired."

He had missed this evening's visiting hours, but there were visiting hours again in the morning. It seemed crazy to drive all the way back to Culver Creek and then back here again in the morning, when he could just spend the night crashing here.

"Thanks, again," Sage said.

"No problem," Rod said. "You going to be okay?"

"Yeah," Sage said, but he knew he didn't sound totally convincing.

24

A CLEANED-UP, patched-up Justin signed the form the billing assistant handed him.

"Okay, Mr. Chandler," she said with a smile. "You're good to go."

He smiled back at her. "I was wondering if you could point me in the direction of the restroom."

Justin limped off in the direction she pointed. When he was sure she wasn't watching him anymore, he made a sharp turn to the right and went down the hallway to the elevator bank. He looked around nervously, but no one tried to stop him.

He had gotten Kelly Dorian's room number earlier while waiting to be seen by a doctor. He had called the main desk from his cell phone and claimed to be calling from a florist's shop. The kind woman who answered had been more than happy to tell him which room number he should address his delivery to.

As he rode the elevator up to the third floor, he grew nervous. What if her son was there? Justin's sore face hurt just thinking about that man, but no, he wouldn't be there. The police had arrested him. But Justin couldn't help thinking of Virgil Chandler. The police had let him go. What was to stop them from letting Sage Dorian go as well?

He tried to project confidence as he walked down the hall to avoid arousing suspicion, but still he slowed his pace as he neared Kelly Dorian's door. It was a bad idea to have come up here, he realized, but this was something he needed to do.

The door to her room was ajar. He leaned his head in and saw her sleeping in the bed surrounded by a maze of tubes. Then he gasped. She wasn't alone. A man lay on a cot wedged between her bed and the wall, and he was awake.

"May I help you?" the man asked.

"I have the wrong room?" Justin said, but it came out like a question. He glanced back toward the nurses' station, but no one seemed to have taken notice of him. He made no attempt to leave the doorway, and the man on the cot regarded him with confusion. *Her husband.* The words were only a whisper in his head, and he wasn't sure if it was the voices or just a hunch, but he felt instantly sure that was who the man must be.

Justin remembered that he looked like someone who had wound up on the wrong end of a battering ram, and he knew that was probably making this man nervous, but his feet felt like they had become rooted to this spot. He had intended to deliver his message to Kelly Dorian, but he supposed it could just as well be delivered to her husband, Melodie's father.

"No," Justin said. "This is the right room."

"Sir?"

The voice came from behind him. Justin glanced back and saw it was a nurse.

"Sir, you can't be in here," she said.

Justin ignored her.

"I just wanted to say I'm sorry," Justin said to Mr. Dorian, the man in the cot.

"Sir, visiting hours are over," the nurse said. "Do you have a pass?"

"I just wanted to say I'm sorry for everything," Justin told the bewildered man.

He had more to say, so much more. But a hand grabbed his sore shoulder, and he flinched.

"Okay, let's go," said a deep voice in his ear, and a big, burly security guard began to walk him down the hall.

"I need to tell them," Justin said.

"Visiting hours resume in the morning," the guard said. "You can tell them then."

But Justin knew they were never going to let him in to see Kelly Dorian.

25

SAGE AWOKE to a yelp of surprise. He blinked open his eyes to see a woman he didn't recognize staring down at him. It was his turn to yelp. He could tell by the way his back felt that he had fallen asleep on the couch again, but as he looked around, he realized that wasn't quite right.

He had fallen asleep on *a* couch, but not his couch. And then the stiff soreness in his hand brought the events of yesterday back to him with disturbing clarity—beating the crap out of Virgil Chandler, getting arrested, and then crashing at his mother's empty house.

No, wait, that hadn't been Virgil Chandler. According to Briggs, the guy he beat up was named Justin Turner. There was something important about that. Something that nagged at him, but what?

"What are you doing here?" He turned and saw Zoey Wilson standing in the living room doorway, dressed in her real estate agent clothes. She was not alone. A middle-aged couple was with her, one of whom he realized had been peering at him a few seconds ago.

"I stayed here last night," he said. "I didn't realize you had a showing."

She waved the couple in to check out the kitchen and promised she would be there in a second.

He studied her, his half sister. She looked nothing like him, nothing like his sister, nothing like his mother. Was it possible he was mistaken? But he had seen the lab report Giselle showed him. Of course, DNA wasn't infallible. Zoey's dad had been serving a life sentence because of faulty DNA testing. Sage felt that nagging thought again in his not fully awake brain.

"Don't you own pants?" she asked.

He looked down and saw that he was wearing only his boxers and an old souvenir T-shirt from Ocean City, Maryland. He recalled his decision to toss his clothes in the washing machine in the hopes of washing off some of the dirt and grime they had acquired during yesterday's eventful day. He must have fallen asleep before he got a chance to toss them into the dryer.

"What time is it?" he asked.

"Quarter to eleven," she said.

"I've got to go," he said. Visiting hours would be over soon.

"Put on some pants," she advised. "And you might want to run a brush through your hair." That was it—the nagging thing that had been bothering him.

"Your brush!" he yelled.

This drew the husband out from the kitchen.

"Everything okay?" Clearly he was checking on Zoey to make sure the crazy man who had been found sleeping on the couch in his underwear wasn't attacking her.

"Fine," she said to him with a tight-lipped smile. "I'll be right there." She waited until he went back into the kitchen to say to Sage in a hissed whisper, "What is wrong with you? I'm trying to sell your mother's house here."

"We're not related," he said with a jubilant laugh. "The hairbrushes were switched."

He was referring to the old police report from her father's arrest. The police investigating the murder of one of his students had collected hairbrushes from each of the family members to check DNA samples, but when Zoey had been going through the old report, she noticed they had mixed up her brush and her sister's brush.

"So that means my murderer sister is your half sister?" Zoey asked.

Sage realized this must be true, and disturbed as he had been to learn that he and Zoey might be related, he was now more disturbed to find out Arielle was actually his half sister. Not only was she a murderer, she was a defense attorney.

"I guess so," he said. In his mind, he saw Arielle berating him in a courtroom as she defended a murderer client. He felt sick to his stomach to think he was related to that woman.

"So does that mean my dad isn't really her father?" Zoey asked.

"I think we need to talk to your mother," he said, "but first I need to go visit mine."

H is mother's condition was unchanged. He stood there staring at her as the machines keeping her alive hummed away. Beside the bed was a fold-up cot with a tangle of blankets atop it. His father was nowhere in sight.

"Looks pretty nasty."

Sage looked up to see the doctor had stepped silently into

the room. The doctor nodded at sage's hand. It was swollen slightly, and dark bruises had formed.

"It's nothing," Sage said, instinctively shoving his hand into his pocket.

"I'd hate to see the other guy," the doctor said with a little laugh, and Sage offered up a fake chuckle in response.

"How is she?" Sage asked.

"About the same," the doctor said. "Now it's just a waiting game."

"In your opinion, what do you think her chances are?" Sage asked.

"Her condition is stable, and that's a good thing."

It was no kind of answer. It sounded like the sort of thing a politician might say, and he loathed politicians even more than defense attorneys.

"Look," the doctor said, giving Sage his full attention, "I can tell she has a loving and supportive family, and in my experience, that's the most helpful thing of all for someone in this condition. She has a reason to want to wake up. It's not a guarantee that she will, and it's not a scientific fact, but anecdotally, I'd say that's one of the most important things."

Sage knew the words were meant to reassure him, but they did just the opposite. A few minutes later, as he walked down the hospital corridor, he couldn't help but think of all the reasons his mother had to not want to wake up. Her daughter, who was arguably the kindest, most loving member of her family, was gone. Her son had been refusing to return her phone calls for weeks. Plus, there was the fact that for years she had been harboring a secret, and maybe she suspected Sage had discovered it. The way Sage looked at it, his mother had a whole lot of reasons *not* to want to wake up.

～

As Zoey drove him to her mother's condo, Sage did his best to explain how he discovered his dad was not actually his biological father, a discovery his sister had also made, just before she was killed.

"I wonder what made her decide to do the DNA test," Zoey said.

"Maybe she had an interest in genealogy," Sage said.

"Yeah, but then she would just test her own DNA," Zoey said. "Not your father's."

She made a good point, and Sage was silent as he considered this. What had led her to do the DNA tests? Had his mom confided in her? Sage felt a bit jealous of his dead sister. Realized this was ridiculous, he shook off the feeling. Besides, he doubted his mother would have said anything. Why suddenly tell Melodie the secret she had been holding on to for years. It didn't make sense. Unless she had said something by accident, or maybe his father had.

"Listen," Zoey said as she turned into the condominium parking lot. "My mother can be a bit touchy about things. So probably it's best to let me handle the talking."

"I'm fully capable of having a conversation with someone," Sage assured her, but for a moment he saw himself raining down blows on Virgil or Justin or whatever the hell that guy's name was.

"That's not what I heard from my father," Zoey said, and Sage recalled how royally he had screwed up that interaction as well. Maybe he would let Zoey take the lead on this one.

A few minutes later, he and Zoey were sitting in the living room of her mother's condo, a huge space that was lavishly decorated. Sage estimated the couches alone cost more than he made in a year—well, more than he had made in a year when he was gainfully employed.

Sage's mother stepped into the room carrying three filled martini glasses on a tray and began to pass them out.

"None for me, thanks," Sage said, but Nan Masterson waved away this protest.

"Nonsense, there's nothing wrong with an afternoon drink, I always say." She handed the drink to him. "I'm just surprised Zoey didn't tell me she was seeing anyone new. She never tells me anything."

Sage thought this was interesting coming from a woman who had been keeping a secret from her daughter her whole life.

"Oh, we're not—" Sage started to say, but Zoey cut him off.

"We've only just started dating," Zoey said.

"Zoey said on the phone that you're a researcher at a university," Nan said.

Sage looked alarmed. Zoey hadn't told him about this lie, and he felt a bit flat-footed.

"I never said he was at a university," Zoey said. "Mom, don't put—"

"All I know," Nan said, "is that I'm glad some of your sister is starting to rub off on you. Zoey's always had questionable taste in men."

Sage looked over and saw Zoey's face redden, but what shocked Sage was the fact that Nan seemed to think Arielle rubbing off on Zoey was a good thing. Her older daughter was a murderer. Her last victim was Zoey's previous boyfriend. So the comparison was especially shocking.

Without thinking, he took a sip from the drink in his hand. It had been six years since he touched alcohol, and the strong drink was a shock. He sputtered a bit but recovered quickly. That first sip awakened a thirst he hadn't realized he had, and he took another, relishing the taste and the almost instant mellowing it produced. He looked over at Zoey, who had also taken a few sips of her drink, and he wondered if that was how she was able to recover so quickly from her mother's insensitive remark.

"Sage has been doing genealogy research," Zoey said, "and he made a surprising discovery when looking into his own family's DNA."

"Ooh, anyone famous in your family tree?" Nan asked. "My own family's got a family tree that goes all the way back to the *Mayflower*."

"Well, this connection is much more recent," Zoey said. She took another sip of her drink before dropping her bombshell. "Sage has learned that he's related to Arielle."

"Huh, is that something," Nan said, but her tone had changed, and Sage noticed the way she tightened her grip on the martini glass. Her manicured fingernails glinted in the sunlight streaming in through the huge wall of windows. "I'm sure it must be a distant relation."

"They're half siblings," Zoey said.

"Oh," Nan said. "I'm sorry, Sage, what did you say your last name was again?"

"Sage doesn't know who his biological father is," Zoey said. "We're hoping you could enlighten us."

"Well, it would have to be your father, wouldn't it?" Nan asked.

She was trying for a light and airy tone, but her voice was strained, and Sage half expected the glass in her hand to burst from how hard she squeezed it.

"Mom," Zoey said, "we already know Arielle has a different father than me. We just want to know who he is."

"You know what?" Nan said, standing up. "I could use a refill, and Sage, it looks like you could too."

Sage looked at the glass in his hand, surprised to see it was empty. Nan plucked it from his hand and retreated into the kitchen.

"Maybe this was a mistake," Sage whispered to Zoey. "She seems pretty upset."

"She has no right to be," Zoey said, making no effort to lower her voice. "She's the one who's been lying about this for years."

A minute or so later, Nan returned and delivered a full martini glass to Sage before sitting down with her own glass and then draining half of it in a single gulp. Sage had intended to leave his second drink untouched but decided it couldn't hurt to take just one more sip.

"The thing is, I can't talk to you about this," Nan said.

"Give me a break," Zoey said. "I know you're not the delicate flower you pretend to be."

"No," Nan said. "I mean, I'm legally not allowed to talk about it."

"What the hell's that supposed to mean?"

"She signed an NDA," Sage said, surprising himself with the outburst. It earned him an annoyed look from Zoey.

"He's right," Nan said. "I signed a nondisclosure agreement years ago."

"Why would you do that?" Zoey asked.

"I didn't really have much choice," Nan said. "Plus, I needed the money."

"Wait, didn't you used to work for a law firm?" Zoey asked. "Couldn't you have gotten one of the lawyers to help you fight that thing?"

"Then I wouldn't have gotten anything," Nan said.

As the alcohol started to lubricate things inside his head, Sage realized something that Zoey, attacking her mother like a little terrier, hadn't.

"What law firm?" Sage blurted out, earning him another look of reproach from Zoey.

"I'm sorry?" Nan said.

"What law firm did you work for?" Sage asked.

"Cutter, Mackenzie and Hoyle," Nan said, her voice quiet. "That was all a long time ago."

Sage recognized the name right away. He went to take another sip of his drink and was surprised to find that once again he had drained his glass. How had that happened?

In his mind he could see the little Post-it Note with the law firm's name on it that was stuck up on his apartment wall.

"I'm sorry," Sage said, setting his drink down on the coffee table and standing up. The wooziness hit him suddenly, and he swayed on his feet. He had to grab hold of the chair for support. "We need to go."

Zoey looked at him as if he had lost his mind.

"But we didn't—" she began.

"We need to go," he repeated, but this time in a firm and serious tone to stress the urgency.

26

WHEN SAGE STEPPED into his mother's hospital room during evening visiting hours, a nurse was in there, just finishing checking on her. The cot was still empty, but Sage noticed the blankets atop it had been straightened.

"Have you seen my father?" he asked the nurse.

"I think he went down to the cafeteria to get some dinner."

Sage nodded. He turned to head back in the direction of the cafeteria.

"Your parents must have a very good marriage," the nurse called after Sage. "I can see how close they are."

Sage resisted the urge to laugh out loud.

"You have no idea," Sage said.

As he made his way to the cafeteria, Sage realized the nurse wasn't the only one who was clueless. He didn't know the first thing about his parents' marriage. He used to take it for granted that his parents would be together forever. Then, after Melodie's murder, things had gone sour for them, and they had formally separated. Sage had always blamed his sister's murder for his parents' relationship hitting the rocks.

Now, though, he realized it must have been strained well before that. How else to explain that his dad wasn't his actual father? He tried to picture the scenario in which his mother would have had an extramarital affair. Just thinking about that made him sick to his stomach.

He scanned the cafeteria and found his father sitting alone at one of the tables with a tray of food in front of him. His father was staring off into space as if he had forgotten all about eating his meal.

"Sage," his dad said when he went over to the table. "Did you eat yet? Want something?"

Sage shook his head. He wasn't hungry.

"I don't blame you," his dad said. "This food is pretty awful."

"The doctor said there hasn't been any change," Sage said. "I mean, I guess it's good that she's not getting worse, right?"

His dad shrugged.

"You been here this whole time?" Sage asked.

"I went home for a little this morning to have a shower and take a little nap," his dad said. "But I couldn't really sleep."

"Can I ask a question?" Sage asked. His dad shrugged. "Why are you hanging out here round the clock when the two of you can barely stand each other?"

"Is that what you think?" his dad said. "Don't you know I love that woman more than life itself?"

"But she doesn't love you?"

"Things have been strained between us for a while," his dad said. "I've made some terrible mistakes."

"The way I look at it, she's the one who made the mistake," Sage said. "She cheated on you. Twice."

"Do we really need to have that conversation here, now?" his dad asked.

"Well, we need to have it at some point," Sage said. "I'm not the one who's been putting off having it for years."

"Right," his dad said. "Well, it's complicated."

"Doesn't look all that complicated to me," Sage said. "She cheated on you, and the man she had an affair with likely murdered Melodie or had someone do it for him."

"What?" His father looked up in alarm.

"It's a possibility, a real possibility."

"But you don't know that."

"I'm working on gathering some evidence," Sage said.

"Right, well, in that case, I need to correct you on something."

Sage raised his eyebrows skeptically.

"Your mother never cheated on me," his dad said.

"I've got the DNA results," Sage said. "I know you're not really my father, and since I was born two years after you two got married, it follows that Mom was screwing around behind your back."

"Jesus," his dad said. "Don't talk like that. Look, you weren't born two years after we got married. We didn't get married until Melodie was six months old."

"But your anniversary," Sage stammered. "And there's pictures, I've seen pictures of you with me when I was a baby."

"I've known your mother a long time," his father said. "We were friends long before we got married. Sometimes I think about that, how different it would be if we had started dating when we were younger. If we had gotten married before, well, it would have spared her a lot, I think, but then I think how you and Melodie wouldn't have ever been born, and that's not a world I would want to live in."

Sage shook his head as he took in his father's words. "It's like my whole life is a lie."

"Don't say that."

"No, really, everything I know about my childhood, about my parents, it's all a lie. Why would you do that?"

"That wasn't my decision," his dad said. "Your mother had her reasons for keeping some truths from you. It's something you should talk to her about."

"Kind of hard to do that now," Sage said.

"Well, when she wakes up," his dad said.

"If she wakes up," Sage said.

"When," his father repeated.

The law firm name Cutter, Mackenzie and Hoyle was written on a Post-it Note in Sage's apartment because before he had gone into politics, Mick Hillman had been a lawyer at the firm. The firm was a large one. Many lawyers had worked there over the years, but only one of them was the father of the boy his sister was secretly dating at the time of her murder.

Earlier today, Zoey had asked him what prompted Melodie to test her and their dad's DNA. Sage didn't know the answer, but he thought Mick Hillman sharing with her the fact that he was her real father would be a reason to run out and buy some DNA testing kits.

But would Mick Hillman voluntarily share such information with her? He would if he wanted her to break things off with his son. The only problem was that this was a man who had gone to great lengths to keep his illegitimate children a secret.

Zoey's mom had signed an NDA agreement and had been paid for her silence. Had his own mother done the same? Was that why she had never told him or Melodie the truth? Would a man who insisted the women he had affairs with sign an NDA agreement divulge information about her parentage to Melodie?

He would if his plan was to murder her. If Mick Hillman

was his and Melodie's real father, that put him at the top of Sage's suspect list.

"All I want to know is if it's Hillman," Sage said. His father refused to meet his eye. "Is Mick Hillman my father?"

"Why does it matter?" his dad asked.

"You know Melodie was dating his son?" Sage asked. "Yeah, that's right. She had a secret boyfriend none of us even knew about, and because our parents couldn't tell us the truth, she might have been dating her half brother."

"That's a pretty big leap," his dad said.

"Is it?" Sage asked.

"I should get back upstairs," his father said. "I don't like leaving her alone for so long."

Sage's frustration turned into rage, and he fought to keep it tamped down. Now was not the time to explode at his father.

"I could use a walk to stretch my legs," his dad said. It was not a pleasant day for a walk. The sky was overcast and there was a stiff wind, but Sage humored his father by accompanying him on a walk around the hospital's parking lot.

"Your mom and I were friends since we were kids," his dad said. "She was always serious and studious, and I have to admit, I was kind of the opposite. When we were in college, I asked her out a few times, but she turned me down. She wanted to focus on her education, and she didn't appreciate my wild streak."

"You always said you two dated in college," Sage said.

"A white lie," his father said. "Environmental law, that's what your mother was interested in. She wanted to go to law school after she graduated."

"Mom, a lawyer?" Sage had no fondness for the law profession and could not imagine his mother joining their ranks.

"She landed this internship with a prestigious law firm in Philly the summer after her sophomore year," his dad said. "So she jumped on it. The lawyer she was assigned to work with was a young lawyer who was something of a hotshot."

"Mick Hillman," Sage said.

"He was already married at the time, but he was a charmer and successful, and, well, she fell for him. He fed her the usual lies. Told her he was going to leave his wife for her, that sort of thing. When she told him she was pregnant, he gave her the money for the abortion."

"But she never had an abortion," Sage said.

"I drove her to the clinic," his father said, "but she changed her mind. Her parents, a lot of friends, they thought she was crazy. She told them the dad was just some guy she met at a club, a one-night stand."

"She was still in school when I was born," Sage said. "Why make up a story about graduating school early?"

"It was another white lie," his father said. "That one she told to spare me. She didn't want you to think I was irresponsible, and that because of me she had gotten pregnant when she was still in school."

"Her whole life is a lie." Sage took several huge strides, leaving his father behind. As he tried to wrap his head around this revised story of his mother's life, something nagged at him. He froze and spun around. "Wait a minute. I thought you said things ended between her and Hillman, but he was Melodie's father as well."

"It wasn't easy for her to finish school and also care for a baby, but your mother's a pretty amazing woman, and she managed to do it. Still, law school was looking completely out of her reach, but then came an offer too good to pass up. The firm where she interned was willing to hire her. They had a generous tuition reimbursement program that would have made it possible for her to afford to go to law school. Plus, the building they were in had a daycare center on the ground floor, and employees could take advantage of a generous discount."

"She went back to work for that bastard?" Sage asked.

"It was a big firm. She would be working with a completely different team."

"But let me guess," Sage said. "He came in with his lies and bravado and charmed her off her feet."

His father looked down at his own feet and hesitated before responding. "The firm had an annual Labor Day barbecue each year. It was down at the shore. One of the partners had a place right on the water. She wasn't even going to go, but it was more than just a fun day. It was a networking sort of thing as well. So I volunteered to babysit and convinced her to go."

Sage noticed tears in his father's eyes.

"It's her own fault for falling for that weasel's lines," Sage said. He shook his head in disgust.

"I got a call sometime around one in the morning," his father said. "She was crying so much that it was hard to understand what she was saying, but she begged me to drive down there and pick her up. I didn't hesitate. Just strapped you into your car seat and drove straight there. My heart broke when I saw here there outside the twenty-four-hour diner where she asked me to pick her up. Her dress was torn, her makeup was running down her face, and she had the beginnings of a black eye.

"I asked her what happened, but she refused to talk about it. I said we were going straight to the police station to report it, but she said no, she just wanted to go home. She said no one would believe her anyway because she had dated Hillman before, because she already had a child with the man, and she didn't want to drag you into it."

"That bastard raped her!" Sage screamed loud enough to attract the attention of someone walking across the parking lot.

"She never did want to talk about it," his father said, "and I guess I never felt like it was my place to say anything, but now, well . . ." He looked helplessly back at the hospital, and Sage could see that despite his father's round-the-clock vigil, his old man was starting to lose hope.

"She's going to pull through," Sage said, surprising himself. "She's a fighter, right?"

His dad offered up a half-hearted nod. "She was a different person after that night. I think some of the fight went out of her."

"He had her sign an NDA, didn't he?" Sage said.

"I tried to talk her out of it," his dad said. "But she was going to put the money toward school."

"But she never went," Sage said.

"We had started dating at that point, and at first she said she didn't want to start school until after we got married, then she wanted to wait until Melodie was a little older, and well, eventually she just stopped talking about it."

"Meanwhile that asshole is running his smiling idiot ads on television and has everyone and their brother falling all over themselves to lick his boots."

"Karma will get him one of these days," his father said.

"Karma seems to be taking its sweet time," Sage said. "Maybe it could use a helping hand."

27

"SO ARE we going to talk about this?" Ambrose waved his hand in Justin's direction, and he understood that he meant Justin's appearance.

His bruises had only grown uglier since being discharged from the hospital, and though he was still a bit sore, he looked far worse than he felt.

"Some guy went nuts and attacked me," Justin said. "That's hardly my fault."

"Why am I having trouble believing that?" Ambrose asked.

He needs to keep an eye on his little girl, the voices said with an urgent tone.

"Maybe because you're not very observant," Justin said. The voices urgently chattered about Ambrose's kid, but if Justin said something, it would go over the wrong way with his skeptical caseworker.

"I'm going to have to include something about this in my report," Ambrose said.

"I'm the victim here," Justin told him. "I'll get you a copy of the police report."

"Are you telling me you did nothing at all to provoke this man?"

Justin thought back to what happened. He had been driving past Melodie's house, thinking of that night six years ago. Melodie and his mother had died on the same night, but the shocking murder of a sixteen-year-old girl was the story that dominated the newspapers. The middle-aged woman who got hit by a bus became nothing but an afterthought. Strange how things worked out.

Sage was Melodie's brother. Justin knew that from the news stories. He hadn't been returning his mother's phone calls. Justin didn't know what that was about. What he did know was that Sage was a troubled and angry man. He could relate. He had been there himself.

"He thought I hit his mother in the head with a brick," Justin explained.

This got Ambrose's attention. His eyes looked like they were ready to fall out of his skull.

"You threw a brick at someone?" he asked.

"No," Justin said. "I said he thought I threw a brick at her. He was wrong, but he thought I hit her in the head."

"And what gave him this impression?" Ambrose asked.

"Like I said, he was kind of crazy."

Ambrose did one of his big sighs.

"Virgil, do you think you're the best person to be diagnosing someone else's mental fitness?"

"The whole reason I was there was to see if his mother was okay," he said. "I had talked to her, and I knew she was in danger."

"Haven't we spoken about this?" Ambrose asked. "People don't want you to protect them because you think something bad is going to happen to them."

Justin understood that, he did, but he didn't know how to

get that message across to the voices. He would gladly never give anyone a warning again if it meant he could have some sort of normal life, but that wasn't how it worked. If he didn't try to help them and deliver the important messages, he was the one who had to face the wrath of the voices.

"I'll have them send you a copy of the police report." Justin got up from his seat.

"Okay," Ambrose said. "Fine."

Justin stepped out of the office. He closed the door after him and started down the hall but had to stop before he went too far. The voices were still frantically chattering. He knew what he needed to do. He returned to the caseworker's office.

He stuck his head in the doorway and said, "Your daughter is in danger. You need to watch out for her."

"I don't have a daughter," Ambrose said.

Justin caught a glimpse of his bruised face as he got into his car, and he remembered his terror as Sage mercilessly pummeled him. He had seen the look of fury in the man's eyes and recognized it. He knew what it was like to feel that anger driving your actions.

He had felt the same way, the day he came home from the community college's financial aid office. His application had been turned down. The counselor had explained it was due to too many problems with his credit report.

"We do our best to work with students," she explained, "but I'm afraid, Mr. Turner, in this case, there's not much we can do."

Though the college's rates were reasonable compared to going to a private university or even a state college, they were still way beyond his means. He came home to another overdue notice from the mortgage company. At Officer Briggs's urging, Justin had called to try to work out a payment arrangement with the bank due to extraordinary circumstances, but he had heard the same thing he did from the financial aid counselor. His atrocious credit report raised too many red flags.

He slammed his fist down on the kitchen counter in frustration. The atrocious credit report was not his fault. He had never had a single credit card in his life, but there were credit cards with his name on it, and lots and lots of things that had been purchased and never paid for. Someone was out there living the good life, and Justin was paying the price, and that someone was Virgil Chandler.

Justin's life was a shambles, and he knew exactly who was responsible. Fired up by rage, he decided it was time to track down his nemesis.

28

EVERY TIME he drove past the Pleasant Oaks office building that housed Mick Hillman's campaign headquarters, Sage felt a sense of revulsion. He felt that tenfold as he stepped through the doors and into a room filled with staffers and volunteers busy working on mailings and making phone calls.

"I need to talk to Mick Hillman," Sage said.

Heads swiveled toward him, and the room went silent. Fear and concern rippled through the room, and he knew he must look as wild and out of control as he felt.

"Do you have an appointment?" a young woman asked him. She looked like she was in her twenties. Sage saw what looked to be the very beginnings of a baby bump, and he couldn't help wondering who the father was, and if she too would soon be signing her own NDA.

"Tell him it's Sage Dorian," Sage snapped.

The young woman looked over to a man about her age and nodded at him. He put down what he was working on and went down a hallway. Sage waited impatiently. A few minutes later, the young man returned and stood beside the woman, facing Sage.

"I'm sorry, but Mr. Hillman is unable to meet with you right now. He said you can call his secretary and set up an appointment." The young man tried to hand Sage a business card, but Sage shoved it away. If he tried setting up an appointment with Hillman through his secretary, the politician would always be too busy to meet with him.

"Yeah, well, you can tell that chickenshit bastard he's going to talk to me whether he likes it or not."

The two staffers exchanged looks of concern.

"Go on," said Sage when neither of them made any attempt to move. "Go tell him."

"Sir," the young woman said, "I think it would be best if you left now. Perhaps you would like to put your concerns in a letter."

"I'm not going anywhere, and I'm not writing a letter," Sage said.

The young man shifted nervously, but the young woman had pulled out her phone and looked to be typing a text.

Sage decided to take matters into his own hands. He didn't know where in the building Hillman's office was, but he had seen the way the staffer went and decided to head in that direction. He pushed easily past the two young sentries.

"Sir!" the woman called after him. "Sir, you can't go back there!"

Sage ignored her. He went down a hallway, glancing in the doors as he went, but he had only made it past three empty offices before his path was blocked by a more serious and considerably larger sentry. There was something familiar about him.

"You are not permitted back here," the security guard said. His words were polite, but his tone wasn't. He shifted his jacket ever so slightly, revealing a holstered gun. The firearm triggered Sage's memory. The last time he had seen this man was the night he showed up at the Pleasant Oaks Country Club during Hillman's fundraising dinner.

Sage held up his hands and was preparing to show himself back out when he heard someone call his name. From the other end of the hallway a familiar figure approached, Colin Hillman. The senator's son gave Sage a friendly smile in greeting.

"Ted, it's fine," Colin said to the security guard. "Sage is a friend. I've got this under control."

The security guard looked uncertain, but Colin waved him off. Colin threw a friendly arm around Sage and led him back down the hall.

"Sorry about the security," Colin said. "Everyone's a little bit on edge. There was an incident."

Colin led Sage into a small office and showed him to one of the chairs, claiming the seat behind the desk for himself. Behind him, the office's lone window was patched up with a piece of cardboard, reminding Sage of his mother's kitchen window.

"Was that the incident?" Sage asked, and when Colin nodded in confirmation, Sage asked, "Did someone throw a brick?"

"Worse," Colin said. "Took out the window with a shotgun. Lucky for me, I was taking a coffee break."

"You're a lucky guy," Sage said.

"You probably think I'm the biggest tool."

"No," Sage said. "Not at all."

"Yeah you do," Colin said. "You're just too polite to say it. I know how it looks, me working on my father's campaign, getting paid by Daddy, like I can't hack it out there in the real world."

Sage wanted very badly to dislike Colin Hillman, but he

found that this was difficult to do. The guy was affable, and not in a phony way like his politician father. In fact, Colin seemed almost like the exact opposite of his father, something that made Sage wonder just how much DNA really shaped someone's identity.

"You know, the truth is I'm not even such a big supporter of his," Colin said. "Politically, I mean. How much of a hypocrite does that make me, huh?"

"You gotta do what you gotta do," Sage said. He wasn't even sure what the hell that meant, but he wanted to keep the conversation light and stay in Colin's good graces, at least until he could find out exactly how much Colin knew.

"Easy for you to say," Colin said. "You're a cop, a real live hero."

"I'm afraid not everyone out there shares that all-cops-are-heroes opinion," Sage said.

"Well, you're a hero in my book," Colin said. "I wish I had chosen to do something more heroic with my life. Instead I'm sitting here in this stupid office sending out press releases and glad-handing reporters."

In all actuality, Sage wasn't a cop anymore thanks to Mick Hillman using his influence to get Sage fired, but clearly that information had not been shared with Colin. It gave Sage an idea.

"Actually, the reason I'm here is because of a serious matter," Sage said. "We have reason to believe Mick Hillman's offspring may be in danger."

"That's a weird way to put it," Colin said. "I mean, you must know I'm Mick Hillman's only offspring."

"Are you sure about that?" Sage gave Colin a serious look, and for the first time since he had stepped into the press office, Colin's friendly face drooped. "Mick Hillman had at least two illegitimate children," Sage continued, "and both of them have been murdered."

Sage was taking a lot of liberties with his statement, but he still feared that Colin could throw him out at any moment, and he didn't want to mess around with ifs, maybes and speculations.

"So you think there's someone who wants to murder me roaming around out there?" Colin asked.

Sage wasn't so sure about that, but there was the matter of someone shooting a gun into this office. At a time when Colin, conveniently, wasn't in it, Sage reminded himself. It was kind of a classic way to draw attention away from yourself as a suspect, wasn't it? Making it look like you, too, were a target.

"You or maybe one of your half siblings," Sage said.

"Half siblings. You're saying I've got more family out there I've never met?"

Sage thought back to the moment he had seen those DNA test results, a few weeks ago, when he learned his father was not his biological father. He had half expected it, and still his mind was blown. The information had pretty much knocked him on his ass. Shouldn't Colin Hillman be having a similar reaction if this was his first time learning he had some half siblings out there? Granted, it wasn't quite the same thing as learning a shocking revelation about the man you thought was your dad, but it was still pretty huge, and Colin seemed unfazed. Sage couldn't help but wonder if none of this was news to Colin.

An only child finding out that his father had illegitimate children out there should come as a bit of a shock. Maybe for Colin it had led to feelings of jealousy. Wouldn't that be natural for a spoiled, only-child rich boy like him? Maybe jealous Colin had taken steps to eliminate these half siblings, one by one.

"I don't know," Sage said. "Why don't you tell me?"

Colin gave a little bark of a fake laugh and shook his head. "Listen, if my father had some other kids out there, I would be the last person he would tell."

"You ever do one of those DNA test things?" Sage asked.

Colin's face went pale, and he stared at Sage with narrowed eyes. Sage figured he was seconds from being shown the door. Still, he studied Colin, looking for the telltale clue that all of this was some act, that the man sitting before him was the homicidal maniac who had killed his sister.

"Did she tell you about that?" Colin asked.

"Who?" Sage asked.

"Melodie," Colin said. "We had a little bit of a fight about that. I mean, nothing major, but I always wondered if that was the reason she broke up with me. It really seemed to matter to her."

"Melodie wanted you to do a DNA test?" Sage asked. So she had known. This proved it, in his mind, and if Colin was telling the truth, then he wasn't the one who had told her.

"Yeah," Colin said. "She bought us each one of those kits. She said it would be fun to find out about our ancestry and stuff. I was busy with school. I was getting ready for my semester abroad and had a lot of stuff to do." Colin paused and looked toward the patched-up window before returning his attention to Sage. "No, that wasn't really it."

Dissatisfied with his lack of a view, Colin turned to the wall where a map of the state of Pennsylvania was hung, and though his gaze was on Altoona, Sage figured what he was seeing was something much further away. After a minute or so, he turned back to Sage.

"It may sound strange for someone who has had to live so much of his life in the spotlight thanks to his politician father, but I'm kind of a private person, and I don't like the idea of just sending my DNA out there to some random company. You ever read the fine print on one of those DNA tests? You have to give up a lot just to find out that your great-grandmother was born in the south of France."

"So you never did the test?" Sage said.

"Still have the original box," Colin said. "After Melodie . . . after . . ." He waved his hand in the air to indicate murder. "Well, I felt awful about being stubborn about that dumb test. I mean, maybe if I had done it, she would still be here."

There were tears in Colin's eyes, and Sage knew the right thing to do would have been to tell Colin his refusal to do the DNA test was not responsible for Melodie's death.

"She did the test on her own," Sage said. "I found the results with her stuff."

He watched Colin's face, but the man barely flinched. Just nodded in response.

"I'm glad," he said. "I mean, I guess that's something I always regretted. I should have done that stupid test. She was right to break up with me."

"Why do you say that?"

"I was no fun," Colin said. "All serious, thinking about the future and how I was going to follow in my dad's footsteps and be some hotshot lawyer and worried that some DNA test thing could be used against me somehow." Colin shook his head. "What a pompous idiot I was."

"What made you think it could be used against you?" Sage asked. It seemed like a strange decision to come to.

"I don't know," Colin said. "Like I said, I was an idiot. I mean, look at me now, right? I never even finished law school. I'm just some poor schmo who wouldn't even have a job if his father hadn't taken pity on him."

"Melodie never told you why she broke up with you?" Sage asked.

"No, but it's obvious, isn't it? She was this fun-loving, care-free person, and I was nothing but some boring stick-in-the-mud."

"She broke up with you right after she got those DNA test results," Sage said.

Still Colin remained unfazed, and either the man was a very good actor, or he really didn't know. The man looked so sad, and Sage could relate to him. The truth was, he felt a kinship to him. So maybe there was something to that whole DNA connection, after all.

"It wasn't because you didn't take the test," Sage said.

"It didn't have anything to do with that?" Colin asked. "How do you know?"

"I don't know for sure," Sage admitted, "and it's not like it didn't have anything to do with the test. I think she broke up with you because she realized you and she were related."

"What?"

"Melodie was one of your half siblings," Sage said.

This finally produced the reaction he had been expecting earlier. Colin pushed his chair back from his desk as if Sage's words were a battering ram that slammed him in the chest. His head looked like it might explode at any second.

"There's something else," Sage said. Colin seemed to have lost the ability to speak. He just shook his head like he couldn't handle any more news, but Sage continued anyway. "We're half siblings as well."

29

JUSTIN SAW Brick Dick (for this was now the only name he could remember for the local police officer) outside his apartment door as he approached. He froze and considered retreating. It was too late. Brick Dick saw him before he could make his getaway. So Justin tried to play it cool.

"What happened to your face?" the cop wanted to know.

"I was attacked," Justin said. There was no point in lying.

"Maybe by someone who caught you throwing a rock through their window," Brick Dick said.

"That's not what happened," Justin said. It was the truth, but his voice wavered, and it made it sound like a lie. It was all Sage's fault. He had accused Justin of throwing a brick through a window. "What are you doing here?" Justin asked.

"I need a sample," the cop said. "For testing purposes."

"Sample?" Justin had visions of the cop taking his fingerprints or swabbing his mouth for DNA.

"One of your bricks," the cop said.

After, as Justin stared at his half-collapsed bookshelf, he wondered if he should have asked the cop for a warrant. They needed a warrant to take evidence from people, didn't they? He had been caught off guard by the whole thing, and he had been scared. If he hadn't been so frightened, he might have thought this whole thing through better.

He was nervous. There was no reason the brick the cop took should match the one found in his neighbor's car, but that was the whole problem. It could have matched or been similar to that brick. The fact was, the bricks Justin had built his bookshelf from didn't necessarily match each other. They were just a hodgepodge assortment he had salvaged from a few different places. Could one of them by chance be similar to the one found in that car? Sure it could, and wasn't that what corrupt cops did? They could claim his brick and the other one matched, and that would be that.

He did his best to prop up the collapsed bookshelf with an empty cardboard box, but it wasn't quite the right size, and he could see that at best this was a temporary solution. The sad little apartment made him feel uneasy. No, that wasn't what was bringing on the uneasiness.

The local police seemed determined to arrest him for a crime he didn't commit. Sage Dorian was out to get him as well. Justin began to feel like a cornered animal.

He was no stranger to fear. He had spent the last six years living in fear, always feeling like he had to sleep with one eye open, knowing that somehow, one way or another, it was all going to catch up with him.

∼

J ustin had to wake up very early on that morning nearly six years ago. The pancake restaurant where he was meeting Virgil Chandler was in Maryland, a little over two hours away from Justin's home.

Well, what for now was his home. Soon the place would belong solely to the mortgage company who was proceeding with foreclosure. That looming event hardened Justin's resolve.

Even though he was nervous about going through with this plan, he had to. If nothing else, he hoped he would feel some sense of vindication, no matter how small.

After tracking down Virgil Chandler's phone number a week ago, Justin had made a call claiming to be one of Virgil's long-lost relatives.

"We've never met," Justin told him. "But as near as I can figure, we're half cousins. Anyway, this childless aunt died, and she named us both in her will."

"An aunt?" Virgil asked. The man sounded skeptical but interested.

"It's not a lot of money, $38,000 to be exact, but hey, it's a nice little surprise, right?"

Justin had picked the random amount because he thought it would be enough to interest an identity thief like Virgil, but not so much that it would arouse suspicion. It worked, and Virgil suggested they meet up at the pancake restaurant.

As he drove there, Justin wished there really was a dead aunt out there who had left him $38,000. That would solve all of his financial woes.

30

SAGE SAT at his mother's kitchen table, staring at his printout of the list of names Colin had emailed. All of these were women who had worked at the law firm of Cutter, Mackenzie and Hoyle during the time Mick Hillman worked there.

"As near as I can figure, this is a complete list," Colin had said when he gave it to him, "but there might have been others."

Being on the list didn't necessarily prove that these were women who'd had affairs with Mick Hillman, but at least it gave Sage someplace to start. His mother was on the list, of course, but none of the other names meant anything to him.

Only one jumped out at him, not the whole name but the last name. Turner. That was what Briggs had said was the name of the guy Sage beat up, Justin Turner. Turner was a common enough name. There probably was no connection, but he decided it was as good a place as any to start.

After a few seconds of internet searching, Sage found a news article about Shawna Turner being struck and killed by a bus. So much for that lead. Then he felt a chill when he saw the date on the article and reread the first paragraph. Shawna

Turner had been killed the same night his sister had, in the same town. It had to mean something, didn't it?

He scrolled through more search results but didn't turn up an obituary that might have shed more light on who Shawna Turner was or if she even was the same Shawna Turner who had been employed at Cutter, Mackenzie and Hoyle. The only thing he found was a short notice about a funeral service that had been held about a week after her death.

~

The Gartner Funeral Home was a simple brick building in a mostly residential neighborhood. The woman who greeted him when he entered introduced herself as Eloise Gartner and said that she ran the business.

"I inherited it from my father, who inherited it from his," she said.

"This is a long shot," Sage said, "but I was wondering if you could tell me about a funeral held here about six years ago, a woman by the name of Shawna Turner."

Eloise nodded at the name. "Come have a seat." She led him to an empty viewing room, where they each took a seat on upholstered chairs.

"I remember Shawna," Eloise said. "So awful what happened to her. I couldn't believe it when I first heard. I mean, imagine being gifted like that and not being able to see your own death coming. So crazy."

"Gifted?" Sage asked.

Eloise blushed and ducked her head.

"I feel foolish admitting this," she said, "but I was one of her clients. I offered Justin to do her service at no charge. It was the least I could do for a woman who had done so much for me."

Heat rose in Sage's own cheeks. It wasn't embarrassment,

though. This was something else entirely, a feeling of excitement that he was getting closer to finding out the truth about what had happened to Melodie. A ringing noise in his ears threatened to drown out what Eloise was saying, and he had to force himself to listen.

"I can tell by your expression you don't believe in psychics," Eloise said. "That's fine. I mean, most of them are scam artists, but Shawna was the real deal."

"She was psychic?" Sage knew his tone made it sound like he was mocking her. He couldn't help it.

Eloise nodded.

"When I first started seeing her, I was stuck in a pretty bad marriage," Eloise said. "I didn't realize that at the time, though. I didn't know how horrible and dangerous my husband was, but Shawna knew. She warned me. I owe my life to that woman, and the fact that she's gone . . ." Eloise shook her head. "Well, it's just not fair, is it?"

Sage muttered some words of agreement. The truth was, he didn't care so much about Shawna, who was long gone.

"What about her son, Justin?" Sage asked. "Do you know how I could get in touch with him?"

"Unfortunately, no," Eloise said. "And it's strange, because he was supposed to contact me so I could give him any sympathy cards we received. That happens, people sometimes send them after the service when they find out about the passing from someone. I guess he fell on hard times, because I remember seeing his mother's house went into foreclosure."

"You didn't see him after the funeral?" Sage asked.

"Just the one time. The last time I saw him, he took his mother's wedding ring and promised to be in touch."

Sage thought of a young man found burned beyond recognition with a simple, plain diamond ring in his pocket, a young man who if the state police's DNA database was to be believed was his half brother.

"Wedding ring?" Sage asked.

"It was the only personal effect he kept," Eloise said. "I think he wanted it for sentimental reasons. It was a simple thing. It couldn't have been very valuable."

"Would you be able to identify it if I showed you a picture of it?" Sage asked.

"Maybe," Eloise said with a shrug. "It was a long time ago."

Sage pulled out his phone and scrolled through the web sleuth forums until he found the Unknown Suitor thread and then the photo of the ring that was found with the burned man's body. There was an evidence tag attached to it in the photo and scorch marks still on the band.

Eloise flinched when he showed it to her, and then she began scrolling to read the rest of the thread. He took the phone back from her.

"Who did you say you were again?" she asked.

"A distant relative," Sage said.

"Must be pretty distant if you're only now finding out about Shawna dying."

"There's a lot I'm only just finding out about," Sage said.

"Well, that's all I can tell you." Eloise stood up to indicate their conversation was now over.

Sage stood as well and walked out of the viewing room and into the funeral home's entryway with its dark, soft carpeting.

"Did you ever receive any sympathy notes?" Sage asked.

"What?" Eloise said.

"You said Justin was supposed to get in touch so you could give him any sympathy cards that came in. I wondered if you ever received any."

"Just one," she said.

"Do you still have it?"

Eloise seemed to weigh whether or not this was something she wanted to give to a strange man who may or may not be related to her former psychic advisor, then decided it probably didn't matter, because she went back into an office to search for it and returned a few minutes later, handing him a lavender-colored envelope.

The card was in an envelope with no return address. Sage noticed it had already been opened. He slipped the card out. It was a standard store-bought sympathy card. It was signed simply MH. He had no doubt Mick Hillman had sent the card.

"He was a good kid," Eloise said. "I mean a little strange, but what do you expect growing up in a place like that? Then becoming a tall, gawky teenager? Well, I'm sure the kids must have picked on him at school. I guess I regret not doing more to look out for him. I owed his mother that much." The words *tall, gawky teenager* stood out for Sage.

"How old was he?" Sage asked. "Did he become a ward of the state?"

"Oh, no, he was an adult," Eloise said. "I mean just barely, couldn't have been more than eighteen or nineteen. Honestly, I thought he would be okay, but then when that cop came around asking questions, well, I feared the worst."

"You said he was tall?" Sage said. "How tall?"

"Oh, I guess about your height," she said. "That must run in your side of the family."

Sage nodded as he mulled this over. The Unknown Suitor had been about five six, not what anyone would generally describe as a tall man, and certainly nowhere near Sage's six-foot, four-inch frame.

"The police were here looking for him?" Sage asked.

"Not long after the funeral," Eloise said. "A cop came in asking a lot of questions, kind of like you are now."

Had the police thought the Unknown Suitor might be

Justin Turner? Is that what had led them to this funeral parlor? A theory that would have been blown to hell when Eloise told them how tall the young man was.

It didn't make any sense. Shawna Turner had clearly known Mick Hillman well enough for the man to send a sympathy card on the occasion of her death. In a freak coincidence, she had been killed the same night as Melodie, and a young man with a wedding ring like hers had been found murdered in a stolen car, a young man who also happened to be Melodie and Sage's half brother. It was too many coincidences for Sage's liking.

Maybe Eloise wasn't so good at judging height, or in her memory she was confusing Justin and some other young man. After all, it had been nearly six years ago. Memory could be a faulty thing.

31

"I JUST HOPE you gave as good as you got," Lennie said as he leaned over Justin's workstation. It was Justin's first day back at work since Sage's beating, and his bruised face had caused something of a stir with his colleagues.

"It wasn't like that," Justin said. "I was jumped."

"Must have been a real nut to go after a big guy like you," Lennie said.

"Yeah, I think he definitely was," Justin said, but he was careful not to say more. He couldn't help thinking of the conversation he'd had with Ambrose.

"Reminds me of my older brother," Lennie said. "He used to beat the crap out of me when we were kids. Thing is, that only worked when I was smaller than him. I'll never forget the day when I was about sixteen, and I fought back. A couple of punches and he was on the floor wailing for mercy. Turns out he was a complete baby when someone his own size fought him, and that was the last day he ever laid a hand on me. That's what you need to do, Virgil, you need to fight back against these bullies."

Justin nodded while silently wishing his boss would leave him alone. He'd dealt with plenty of bullies in school, both those who fought with fists and those who relied on words and psychological abuse. Back then, he used to wish he had a big brother, someone to look out for him and stick up for him. He hadn't considered the fact that a brother could be a bully as well.

Still, he wondered if even an abusive older brother would have been preferable to the profound loneliness of his childhood. It was a loneliness that had only increased after his mother died. Six years ago, for a brief instant he thought he had found the cure to that loneliness in the form of an unlikely friendship, but like everything in his life, that had been cruelly taken from him.

∾

"So, half cousins, huh?" Virgil said as he sat down across from Justin after an awkward hello between the two strangers.

Justin wondered if the lie about being related had been such a good idea now that he got a good look at Virgil. They looked nothing at all alike. Virgil was small and slight, almost the complete opposite of Justin in every way. He reasoned that half cousins weren't all that closely related so there was no reason to assume they should look alike.

"Yeah," Justin said. "I'm an only child, and my mother's gone. So I was excited to learn I had a relative out there."

"No shit," Virgil said. "My mom's gone too, and I can one-up you. I grew up in the foster care system. I ain't got no one."

Justin found himself feeling bad for the guy sitting across from him, which hadn't been the plan at all. He was here to demand answers to why Virgil had stolen Justin's identity and in so doing had taken Justin's mother from him and ruined his life. The whole point of this meeting was so he could vent his anger and frustrations. Feeling sympathy for this man was just going to mess all that up.

"My mother was hit by a bus," Justin said, and he savored the feeling of rage roiling inside him. "The really terrible thing is that it was all because she thought she was on her way to help me out, but it was all a mistake."

"Fate's messed up," Virgil said. "My mother got all this money from the place she worked because they fired her, and then she went out and bought a bunch of drugs and OD'd. Like, if she had just stayed being poor and they hadn't paid her, she would probably still be here."

"Fate is messed up," Justin agreed. The rage had dissipated once again.

As they sat there eating from overloaded plates of pancakes, they talked about all sorts of things—a popular television show that had just gone off the air, the perfect way to prepare pancakes (so that they were ever so slightly running at the center), what they planned to do with their inheritance, and the subjects and teachers they had hated the most when they were in school.

An hour after the meeting began, Justin still hadn't broached the subject of Virgil's identity-thieving ways, and he had decided he wasn't going to mention it at all. The truth was, he liked Virgil, and for the first time in his life, he felt like he had found true friendship. Virgil was like the brother he had always wanted. Except he wasn't a brother, he was a half cousin, only not really. And now more than ever Justin regretted setting up this meeting under false pretenses because what he wanted more than anything was to hang out with Virgil again.

But to do that, he would need to confess to Virgil that they weren't actually related, and worse, that there was no inheritance. Justin felt sick to his stomach, and it wasn't from eating too many pancakes.

"I'll be right back," he announced suddenly, and practically sprinted to the men's room.

∾

I nstead of driving straight home, Justin made a detour after work and found himself standing in front of the display of DNA testing kits at the electronics store. He hadn't been able to stop thinking about that conversation he'd had with that caller earlier.

∾

"Y ou may find that there's strife with family or loved ones," Justin said as he sat at his desk dutifully reading off his script to the woman on the other end of the phone.

"Oh!" she said. "That makes so much sense. I just did one of those DNA test kits my daughter gave me as a birthday gift, and I learned that I have a half sister who only lives a few towns away. She's a few years younger than me. So that means my father must have had an affair. I was really upset at first. I mean, I guess I still am a little, but now I'm kind of excited to think I have a sister I never knew about."

"I didn't know you could learn things like that from those genealogy things," Justin said. "I thought it was just supposed to tell you what nationalities you were."

"They're so high-tech now," she said. "I mean, it only works because I guess my half sister did one of those tests too. Oh! Do you suppose I might have more half siblings out there? Maybe there are and they just haven't done one of those tests. That would be something, wouldn't it?"

"It would," Justin said. "I guess the only way they would find you is if they did a test themself."

"Or maybe that half sister, the one who took the test, knows who they are. You know what, I think it's time I reached out to her. We're only a few towns apart. It's crazy that we've never met. Thank you so much for this reading, it really helped."

Justin could hear that the woman was getting ready to hang up, so he said quickly, "Well, we have just the thing for your meeting with your half sister. It's our family harmony bracelet, and it just so happens to be on sale this week. It would be perfect for making sure your meet-up is a success, and with this week's special price, you might want to pick one up as a nice gift for your half sister."

"Oh, that is a good idea," the woman said.

32

SAGE HAD SPENT a few nights crashing at his mom's place. Stepping back into his apartment after a couple of days away from it was a rude awakening. He saw it as Rod had seen it. The mounds of papers everywhere, the dirty dishes and empty food containers scattered about. He walked over to his wall of Post-it Notes and tried to keep his blinders on to avoid seeing the chaos all around him, but it wasn't working. He could feel the debris. It seemed to be closing in on him.

He retrieved a black plastic trash bag from beneath the kitchen sink and began a tour of the apartment with the aim of collecting all the trash he could. Take-out containers and snack food bags got tossed into the voluminous black bag. He was about to toss in a diet soda can, when he thought of Ambrose retrieving his cup from the trash, and he walked the can into the kitchen, rinsed it out and deposited it into his recycling bin. He froze.

In the past six years, the only alcohol he had consumed were the martinis he drank while at Zoey's mother's condo. That was why what he saw in his recycling bin made no sense.

It was an empty Jim Beam bottle. He reached in and shifted the bottle to make sure he wasn't seeing things, and noticed something else—two beer bottles beneath it. He jumped back from the bin as if it contained a rabid animal, but the truth was, he would have preferred finding a rabid animal in his kitchen to the empty beer and whiskey bottles.

"Someone's been here," he said aloud. He spun around as if the intruder might be ready to sneak up on him, but of course there was no one there.

He went back into the living room and sat down on his couch. He had made barely a dent in cleaning the place up. His memory called up the look of shock on Rod's face as they stepped into the apartment the day Ambrose had bailed on him. Rod thought Sage had gone full batshit crazy. Sage had seen it in his eyes.

What was more likely? That someone had broken into his apartment, hadn't stolen a thing, had a quick drinking session, then rinsed out the bottles and placed them in his recycling bin, or that he had fallen back into his old drinking ways, drank so much he blacked out and had no memory of the entire incident? Clearly the latter made the most sense, but it frightened him that he had no memory of it.

He thought of his attack on Justin Turner. He could remember the first few punches. Then he remembered being pulled off the bloodied young man, but he didn't remember any of the in between stuff. It was a blur. Less than a blur.

Sage tried to rewind and play back the last week or so, looking for any unexplained missing stretches of time, but the problem was, when you were living in something of a fugue state, consumed with trying to find that one key piece of evidence buried in mounds of papers that would lead you to your sister's killer, you didn't really have a firm grasp on time to begin with. He paused when he reached the memory of his meeting with Ambrose Radcliffe.

Everything about that had been strange. Why had the man taken off when Sage went to go get Rod? Sage recalled looking back and seeing Ambrose taking his paper cup out of the trash and placing it in a plastic bag.

Environmentalism run amok had been Sage's initial thought. The kind of thing you would expect a guy who drove a Prius with a Sierra Club sticker on the back to do, except would a Prius-driving Sierra Club supporter use a plastic bag? Weren't true environmentalists working to get plastic bags banned?

Sage jumped up from the couch. Ambrose wasn't a die-hard recycler. Well, maybe he was, but that wasn't why he fished Sage's coffee cup out of the trash. He stole the cup because he wanted to test Sage's DNA.

It gave Sage an idea. He ran into the kitchen and placed a plastic sandwich bag over his hand, then grabbed a plastic grocery store bag from the cabinet. With the sandwich bag over his hand, he removed the whiskey and beer bottles from the recycling bin and placed them in the store bag.

The empty bottles clanked in the bag as he carried them out to his car.

∼

R od didn't exactly sound pleased when he answered Sage's call.

"Please tell me you didn't beat the crap out of someone again," Rod said.

"No," Sage said. "I need an address for someone. She does some work for a local police department."

"Are you applying for a job there?" Rod asked.

"It's about a personal matter," Sage said.

"Your sister," Rod said, because he knew Sage well enough. "Okay, well, if you promise not to go beat her up, I'll get you her address. Give me her name, and I'll look it up tomorrow."

"I need it before then," Sage said.

"I'm done for the day," Rod said.

Sage tried not to sigh in annoyance.

"Can't you say you left something at the station and run back?" Sage asked. "It won't take five minutes."

"Come on, man," Rod said, but Sage could tell his former coworker was going to do this favor for him.

"I owe you big-time," Sage said.

"That debt of yours is getting pretty big," Rod said.

⁓

G iselle's address was in a small apartment building. One of her neighbors had helpfully propped the exterior door open with a brick. He trotted up the stairs to the third floor and went down the hallway until he came to unit 308, her apartment. There was police tape across the door.

"Can I help you?"

Sage looked up to see a man at the other end of the hallway. He had a toolbox in his hand.

"Is this where Giselle lives?" Sage asked.

The man narrowed his eyes. "Who are you?"

Sage looked again at the yellow tape, the man's demeanor. He didn't like this one bit.

"Hey, how did you get in here?" the man asked. "Did someone buzz you up?"

"Door's propped open," Sage said.

"Goddamn tenants," the man muttered. Sage figured he

was the building manager or the landlord. "How do you know Giselle?"

"I don't really," Sage said, but he had already made his decision. He turned back and began to run down the stairs.

"Hang on!" the manager/landlord called after him. "Stop! The police want to talk to everyone who knew her!"

Sage raced down the stairs, but he heard clear as day the past tense in the man's shout. Knew, not know. He didn't like it one bit.

33

JUSTIN SAW the light bar sticking up above the other cars in his apartment complex's parking lot and swerved back onto the road, testing the old Subaru's handling ability and the patience of the drivers behind him who voiced their displeasure with their horns. The cop car didn't mean it was Brick Dick back to harass him some more. The cops could have been there for any reason, but Justin didn't like the odds.

He was too afraid to go home, and he didn't have the money to pay for a motel room. It looked like he was going to spend the night sleeping in his car. How strange it was that history seemed to be repeating itself.

That day in the pancake restaurant, Justin stepped out of the men's room and was surprised to see their table deserted. Virgil was gone, and so was Justin's jacket. That was strange. He looked around the restaurant but didn't see Virgil anywhere.

Maybe Virgil had gone outside to smoke a cigarette. It was cold, so maybe he had borrowed Justin's jacket. Even as he considered this possibility, he realized it was a long shot. Virgil was a crook, and he had just stolen Justin's jacket and fled the scene.

Still, Justin tried to think the most of his new friend as he ran outside. He scanned the lot but didn't see Virgil. He could have already left, but the parking lot extended behind the building. So Justin walked back there. Only a couple of cars were parked out back, and there was a dumpster that smelled ready for emptying.

"Justin!"

The shout came from off in the distance. Justin looked toward the sound of it, and past a trash-strewn field, he saw two figures on an unpaved road. One wore a hooded sweatshirt with the hood pulled down, obscuring their face. The other wore Justin's jacket. Justin opened his mouth to call out to Virgil, but before any words left his mouth, he watched in stunned horror as the hooded figure drew a gun from their pocket, pointed it at Virgil, and pulled the trigger. Virgil collapsed on the ground. Justin watched, but his jacket and the person who wore it remained completely still.

I just witnessed a murder. The thought was followed by less coherent ones, and Justin became dimly aware of the fact that he was in danger. He had just seen a man murdered, and he was standing out there in the open. If the murderer glanced his way, he would spot him. Justin ducked down, hiding himself behind the stinky dumpster, his heart hammering away in his chest.

He wasn't sure how long he crouched there with his back pressed against the cool metal of the dumpster, but it was long enough for semi-coherent thoughts to return to his brain. He played back everything he had heard and seen from the moment someone called his name. The voice calling out his name did not belong to Virgil. Of that he was sure. It had been the person in the hooded sweatshirt who shouted his name, the murderer. But the murderer had not been looking in his direction, and it seemed they hadn't seen him at all.

The murderer had shouted "Justin!" but it was Virgil they were talking to. That made sense. Virgil had been going around using Justin's name, and apparently while he had been impersonating Justin, he had made someone angry enough to want to kill him. Justin wasn't entirely surprised. Hadn't he set up this whole meeting and driven all the way to this pancake place in Maryland because he was so pissed off at Virgil that he wanted to personally tell the man how upset he was? Someone else, apparently, had wanted to do more than vent their frustrations verbally.

Justin rested his head against the dumpster and closed his eyes as he tried to clear the ugliness he had just witnessed from his brain and tried to contemplate what he should do next.

"There you are, you little shit!"

Justin opened his eyes in alarm and jumped to his feet, but it wasn't the figure in the hooded sweatshirt advancing on him. It was his waitress. She had an unlit cigarette in her hand, and he saw the back door of the restaurant fall closed.

"Here's a tip, asswipe," she said. "If you're going to dine and dash, don't hang out in the parking lot after making your getaway."

"That wasn't what I was doing, honest." Justin held up his hands defensively.

"Yeah, right," the waitress said. "That's why you were out here hiding behind the dumpster."

"No, you don't understand," he said, "I just saw—" Justin glanced back to where he had seen Virgil get shot, but both the murderer and Virgil's body were gone. If he told the waitress what happened, she would only think he was lying, making up some elaborate story to get out of paying his bill. He didn't blame her. He would have thought the same thing.

"Save your excuses for someone who cares," she said. "Now let's go settle up."

As soon as he stepped back into the restaurant, he realized he had a huge problem. His wallet had been in the pocket of his jacket. He reached into his pockets, but it was futile. He didn't have so much as a spare quarter on him. The cashier and the waitress stared at him expectantly.

"My wallet's been stolen," Justin said. It was the truth, but it sounded like a whopper of a lie.

The waitress let out a cackle of a laugh.

Ten minutes later, Justin found himself armed with a mop and a cart of cleaning products so he could scrub the public restrooms and start paying off his debt.

34

SAGE HAD SPENT the better part of the night and well into the morning obsessively checking out his front window every few minutes or so. How long would it take the police to figure out who the mysterious man was that had shown up looking for Giselle and then track him down?

There was a car parked in the street out front that had been there for at least half an hour. Nothing unusual there, except there was someone in the car. He had been sitting in it the whole time. The car was too nice and too German to be a cop car, and since it wasn't a Prius, he figured it wasn't Ambrose, but now he was having doubts. What if Ambrose switched cars because he thought he was being followed?

Sage threw on his jacket and ran downstairs. When he reached the sidewalk, he ran straight toward the car. He didn't want to risk Ambrose getting spooked and driving off. But as he approached the car, Sage didn't think the profile of the man behind the wheel was at all right. Then the man turned his head and Sage got a surprise. It wasn't Ambrose, but he did recognize the man.

Colin Hillman recognized him too and opened his car door before Sage had a chance to knock on it.

"Thank God," Colin said. "I wasn't sure how long I was going to have to wait."

"Wait for what?" Sage asked.

"I need to talk to you," Colin said. "You didn't leave a number, but this is probably better anyway. Less traceable."

That made the hairs on the back of Sage's neck go up. He took a step back and looked around for a potential weapon or a hiding spot.

"What you said about someone trying to murder my father's offspring?" Colin asked. "That's true?"

"It's a possibility," Sage said, but he was distracted. He was still trying to plan his next steps.

"Then there's something you should know about." Colin reached for an item on the passenger seat beside him, and Sage went into a crouch, ready to dive for cover or wrestle his assailant for the gun, whichever seemed best. Colin turned back to face him. There was a piece of paper in his hand. He gave Sage a strange look. "What's wrong?" Colin asked him. "Are you ill?"

"Fine," Sage said, straightening up. Colin extended the paper toward him, and he took it. His mind and his heart rate were still going a million miles a second. It was tough to focus on the words on the page.

"We received a credible tip about another descendent of my father's," Colin said. "The campaign is in full-on damage control mode right now. The news hasn't broken, but it's just a matter of time."

"Oh," Sage said.

"So anyway, you didn't get this information from me," Colin said. "If you claim you did, I'll deny it. But I thought you should know. She's Melodie's age."

Sage had finally calmed down enough to make sense of the words on the paper. He saw a name there, Jillian Werks, and an age, seventeen. When Colin said Melodie's age, he meant the age that Melodie was when she was killed.

"I've got to go," Colin said, and he started up the car. "Just keep her safe. Make sure nothing happens to her."

Without another word, Colin slammed his door and pulled out onto the road. Sage made an attempt to mutter his thanks, but of course Colin couldn't hear it. As he stood there on the sidewalk, he noticed something else on the piece of paper. Jillian Werks lived right here in Culver Creek.

S age sat in his car in the parking lot of a strip mall that was across the street from the Culver Creek High School. To the best of his knowledge, Jillian Werks, the half sister he had only learned about a couple of hours ago, was still inside the building. He had gone to her home address, but no one was there. So he was here waiting for the final bell to dismiss the students so he could talk to the girl directly.

If Colin thought it was important enough to come here and alert him to the girl's existence, then he must sincerely believe the girl's life was in danger. This troubled Sage. Did it mean Colin suspected his father of having Melodie murdered? If Mick Hillman was behind the murders, then Jillian was in trouble. Colin had said the campaign was already in damage control mode.

It was not a matter of if the story about Mick Hillman's illegitimate daughter would break, but when. How far would Mick Hillman go to protect his reputation? How far had he gone already?

The strip mall parking lot afforded Sage a decent view of

the high school as well as the road in front of it which, as the end of the school day neared, had grown crowded with parked cars waiting to ferry the exiting students home or to orthodontist appointments or to whatever extracurricular activities were on the day's agenda. The minivans and SUVs that now filled the street had the look of typical mom vehicles, but Sage eyed them all with suspicion. Any one of them could contain a hired killer waiting to do Mick Hillman's bidding and end the life of a teenage girl. Not for the first time since he had pulled into this lot, Sage wondered if he had done the right thing by coming here alone instead of alerting the police to his concerns.

But Mick Hillman was the reason he was no longer employed with the Culver Creek Police Department, and Sage wasn't sure how far his influence there went. Plus, there was the problem that he didn't have any solid evidence to support this vigil of his. He was here because of a hunch and some information that was shared with him in confidence. Basically, he was a step removed from being a conspiracy theory nutter.

Sage watched as a school bus pulled into the circular driveway in front of the school and took its place at the end of the line of buses. Jillian was seventeen. Would she be taking the school bus home? Maybe one of the cars lined up in front of the school was Mrs. Werks waiting to drive her daughter home. But it was also possible Jillian had a car of her own, or a friend with one, and would head out the side door that led to the student parking lot.

Then the magical hour arrived. The front doors of the school opened, and students spilled forth. Sage realized the utter futility of his plan. Thanks to Instagram, he had found images of Jillian Werks and knew what she looked like, but picking out her face from the hundreds now exiting the high school was nothing short of impossible. He would have been better off waiting for Jillian at her home address.

Within a few minutes, the first in the line of school buses pulled out of the driveway. The mom vehicles began pulling out onto the road as well. Maybe it wasn't too late to get back to Jillian's house in the hope of intercepting her there. He started up his car and joined the fray on the busy road. Horns blared as he cut off a departing mom vehicle, but he paid it no mind. Jillian's house was more than three miles from the school, and he needed to get there, but traffic crawled on the clogged street.

He drummed his fingers impatiently on the steering wheel and craned his head to try to get a look down the street to see how far the traffic jam extended. Would it clear anytime soon? Maybe he should turn around and take the long way to Jillian's house. There was less traffic in the opposite direction, and even though he would be driving out of his way, it might just be quicker.

He looked out his window as he contemplated making an abrupt and very illegal U-turn, and there on the sidewalk he saw something that made his heart race. The girl with the ponytail and the fleece jacket, standing there looking down at her phone, was none other than Jillian Werks. Luck was on his side.

He executed a sudden U-turn and was greeted with a volley of car horns from every direction. The noise caused Jillian to look up from her phone, and there was something in her expression, in the tilt of her head, that made Sage think of Melodie. Could there be any doubt that Jillian was well and truly his half sister?

Sage pulled over to the curb in front of the car and opened his passenger window.

"Jillian!" he yelled.

She looked into his car, her eyes narrowed, but when she

saw only a strange man behind the wheel of a car she didn't recognize, she instinctively backed away.

Sage threw open his door to a renewed chorus of beeping and ran over to Jillian on the sidewalk. She had the panicked look of a deer caught in the headlights.

"Wait!" Sage said. "Don't run. Your name is Jillian Werks, right?"

She nodded slowly.

"I think you might be in danger," he said.

"Who are you?" She still looked panicked, but at least she hadn't run off.

The question was a reasonable one, but he didn't know how to answer it. Did he tell her he was once a cop? Did he tell her he might be her half brother?

"That doesn't matter," he said. "I need to know, have you noticed anyone following you? Has anything strange or suspicious happened today?"

She blinked at him but didn't speak. He had the sudden realization of how this might look to passersby. Here he was, this big hulk of a man, looming over this frightened-looking teenage girl. People driving by might get the wrong idea. He glanced around but saw only folks so wrapped up in their own worlds they were oblivious to the drama unfolding on the sidewalk.

He turned back to Jillian, who was ever so slowly inching away from him. He needed to do a better job of explaining to her why she was in danger. He opened his mouth to speak, but before he did, what he had seen a moment ago finally registered, and he spun back around in time to see a silver Prius pull away from the curb less than a block away and start driving straight toward them, oblivious to the anger this elicited from the other motorists.

"Quick!" Sage shouted. "We have to get out of here! That's him!"

He grabbed Jillian's arm and dragged her toward his car. Her phone fell from her hand and clattered onto the sidewalk. She tried to reach for it, but there was no time.

He pushed Jillian in through the driver's side door, forcing her to climb over the emergency brake so he could get behind the wheel. While she was still struggling to get over the e-brake and into the passenger seat, he hit the gas and they jolted out onto the road.

"Help!" Jillian screamed. "Somebody help me!"

The passenger window was still rolled down, which meant someone must have heard her cries, but he couldn't stop now, not until they were safely away from the Prius. He looked in his rearview mirror, but he'd lost sight of the car.

"I'm helping you," he said. "You have to trust me."

He hit the gas to put as much distance between them and the school as he could. His doors locked with a thwack as they did anytime he hit thirty miles per hour. He looked over, and Jillian had disentangled herself from the emergency brake and now yanked on the handle of the locked door.

"Let me out!" she screamed, too panicked to think of hitting the button to unlock the door.

He checked the mirror again for the Prius. He didn't see it, but what he did see was that behind him, concerned moms were climbing out of their cars and pointing in his direction. If they hadn't called 9-1-1 yet, they would soon. Maybe he hadn't handled things so well, but he couldn't worry about that now. He needed to get Jillian to safety. He would just have to explain everything to her and Culver Creek's finest later.

"Someone wants to hurt you," Sage said. "You have to understand you're in danger."

"Yeah, from you," she said.

As they came up on an intersection, he jerked the wheel to the right and drove them down the side street. He didn't know where he was going, didn't have a plan. Right now, the most important thing was to get away from Ambrose. He could only assume the man was armed. Did he have a gun? At any moment he could open fire on them. That was why it was so important that they got out of range.

Sage spared another glance in the mirror in time to see a flash of silver as a car hung a right turn on the road. Crap. He had caught up to them.

"Watch out!" Jillian screamed.

Sage looked forward and saw cars stopped up ahead. Not good. They couldn't stop. To their right was curb and front lawns. He decided to go for it.

Sage pounded the gas at the same time as he jerked the wheel. The car leaped over the curb, and he kept his foot on the gas as they bounced along on the uneven terrain. It wasn't smooth driving, but his all-wheel-drive vehicle could handle it. He only hoped the Prius wouldn't be able to handle this suburban version of off-roading.

They neared the next intersection, and he cut the corner. The car bounced back over the curb and onto the smooth road surface once again. He pounded on the gas, then executed a sharp left turn when he spotted a street sign at the last second. He hoped he had been quick enough to evade their pursuer. He looked back and saw no one there. That was good. He realized they were not far from the highway on-ramp. If they could make it to the highway, they would have a decent chance of getting away from Ambrose, and Sage would be able to explain everything to Jillian so she understood he wasn't the bad guy.

But he didn't need to wait that long.

"I'm your half brother," he told her.

"What are you talking about?" she asked him.

"Do you know who Mick Hillman is?" he asked.

"Mick Hillman puts Pennsylvania first," Jillian said, quoting one of the campaign commercials that played endlessly.

"Right," Sage said. "He's our real father."

"No, he's not," she said. "You've got the wrong person."

"You're Jillian Werks," he said, because for a split second he had a panicked feeling that he really did have the wrong person.

"Yeah, as in David Werks's daughter," she said.

"Right, but he's not really your dad. Believe me, I was as surprised as you were when I learned my father wasn't my real father."

"But my dad is my real dad," Jillian insisted. "I should know. We look alike. And we both sneeze when it's sunny."

"You just think you're related," Sage said. "Mick Hillman's your real father, and because of that, your life is in danger."

They were almost to the highway ramp, and there was still no sign of the silver Prius behind them. His reckless driving might have been enough to shake off their tail.

"Stop!" she screamed at him.

"I know it's hard to hear, but I'm telling you it's true."

"No," she said. "Stop!"

She pointed out the windshield, and then he saw it too. A police cruiser was parked across the road blocking both lanes. A roadblock. He glanced to the right to see if he might attempt another getaway, but the side of the road fell away into a deep ditch. He hit the brakes, and the car came to a stop a few feet shy of the parked cruiser. At almost the same time, a klaxon warning sounded from Sage's phone. He glanced at where it rested in his cupholder and saw the words "AMBER ALERT" there. Crap.

Jillian fumbled with her door again, but this time she

managed to figure out how to unlock it. She swung the door open and ran from the vehicle in the direction of the cop car. As Sage watched, one of his former colleagues came out from behind the parked cruiser and helped Jillian get safely out of the road and onto the shoulder. She was gesturing in his direction.

Then a familiar voice, amplified by a bullhorn, said, "Please step out of the car with your hands in the air."

Sage sighed, then swung open his door, and with his hands carefully held aloft, he stepped out onto the road.

"Sage?" Rod said, this time without the aid of his bullhorn. "What the hell?"

35

JUSTIN WAS thankful that the truck stop parking lot was crowded. It made it less likely that a car parked there for hours on end would stand out. He wished he had worn a warmer coat, though. He shifted around in the backseat trying to get comfortable. It reminded him of that night all those years ago— his first night as Virgil Chandler.

It was dark by the time he left the pancake place. His hands ached from the bathroom scrubbing and the dishwashing. He smelled of grease and rotten food thanks to all the trash he had hauled out to the dumpster. What he wanted more than anything was to take a long, hot shower, but he couldn't go home.

A wave of grief hit him as he realized he could never go home again. The person who murdered Virgil thought they were killing Justin Turner, and they now had Justin's wallet with his driver's license. If they had examined the thing closely enough, they would have realized that whoever they murdered was not Justin Turner. But the other thing they would have was Justin's address. After disposing of Virgil's body, they probably went straight to Justin's house. The murderer was probably sitting there waiting for him.

Justin was broke, tired and suddenly homeless. He was thankful his mom always kept spare car keys in the glove compartment, and thankful he was so forgetful about locking the car. So he started up her old Subaru and drove out of the parking lot, determined to get as far away from the place as whatever gas he had in the tank would allow.

While scrubbing grimy public bathroom tiles, Justin had too much time to overthink things. If he hadn't spent so much time thinking, he probably would have driven straight to Officer Briggs's house, told him everything that happened and asked for help.

The police can't help you, the voices whispered in his head. *To them, you're a criminal, and that's all you'll ever be.*

As always, the voices were right. Justin had promised Briggs he wouldn't try to find Virgil, but he had gone back on that promise. He had called the man up and fed him some lies to trick him into coming to the pancake place. Then someone had gone and murdered Virgil, but Justin didn't have any sort of physical description of the murderer. He couldn't even say for sure whether it was a man or a woman. Justin knew what would happen when he told his story to Briggs. The cop would no more believe Justin hadn't murdered Virgil than that waitress believed he wasn't trying to run off without paying his bill.

An hour or so after leaving the pancake restaurant, with exhaustion setting in and his gas gauge creeping toward empty, Justin pulled off the highway into a rest area. He longed for his bed or at the very least his jacket on such a cool night, but he would have to settle for the old hooded sweatshirt he found in the backseat. He pulled it over him, yanking the hood over his head for extra warmth, and did his best to get comfortable in the less-than-accommodating car.

36

SAGE WASN'T sure how long he had been locked in the small interview room. It felt like hours. Maybe they had forgotten about him.

When Rod finally walked in, Sage's mood lifted, but that changed when he saw the expression on Rod's face.

"They want to arrest you," Rod said. "And I'm trying to come up with a reason I should talk them out of it."

Rod sat down in the chair across from Sage. The same chair Sage himself used to sit in when he had a suspect to interview.

"Who's they?" Sage asked.

Rod waved his hand in the direction of the door. "The whole department. What were you thinking?" He shook his head, utterly perplexed by Sage's actions.

"She was in danger," Sage explained. "I was trying to save her life."

"By driving like a maniac and nearly killing her in a car accident?"

"Someone was chasing us," Sage explained. "I didn't know if he had a gun."

"Someone was chasing you?" Rod repeated. He sounded unconvinced.

"Remember that guy I wanted you to take a statement from at the coffee shop? The one who took off? It was him."

Rod rubbed at his chin and shook his head.

"We took statements from witnesses," Rod said. "The ones who saw you driving like a madman? None of them mentioned anything about someone chasing you."

"I jumped the curb to get away," Sage explained. "I don't think he could manage it in his Prius."

"Right." Rod nodded, but Sage could tell he was doubtful. "She's the girl you called me about last night."

"Last night?" Sage wondered what Mick Hillman was playing at. Had he called up Rod pretending to be Sage? Sage wondered what could have been said. All he knew was he wasn't the one who called Rod. He hadn't even known about Jillian until this morning. Last night he was trying to track down who had broken into his apartment, and then he remembered he did call Rod. He had wanted Giselle's home address. Giselle, Jillian, the names were close enough that he understood Rod's confusion. "You're thinking of Giselle," Sage said. "That's someone else. That had nothing to do with this."

"I'm not blaming you," Rod said. "You've been under a tremendous amount of stress lately."

"I wasn't calling you about Jillian," Sage insisted because he feared he hadn't done a good enough job of making his point.

"I mean what happened to you, losing your job, well, that just wasn't right," Rod said. "Then with what happened to your mom. What I'm saying is, it's been a lot, I don't blame you."

"Don't blame me?" Sage repeated. "No, you don't understand. I was trying to help her. She's my half sister. Someone's trying to kill her."

"You're related?" Rod asked. "She said she had never seen you before."

"Well, I only found out about her this morning," Sage explained. "Her father's Mick Hillman."

Rod gave a little snicker of a laugh and shook his head again.

"Come on, man," Rod said. "I met her father. He came to pick her up."

"No," Sage said. "He's not her real father. I mean he raised her, but he's not her birth father."

"She's the spitting image of him," Rod said.

Sage thought of what Jillian had said in the car. That she and her dad looked alike and something about sneezing on sunny days.

He had been set up. The more he thought about it, he realized it had to be true. Colin Hillman had come to him and given him Jillian's name, said she was Mick's illegitimate daughter. Claimed to have received a tip about her. But what if the whole thing was bogus? Mick Hillman had gotten Sage fired. Was it that much of a stretch to think he would stoop to pulling a stunt like this to get Sage in trouble?

Sage recalled what else Colin said, that he would deny ever having given this information to Sage. Well, that was convenient, wasn't it?

"I think it was all a stunt," Sage said.

"What was a stunt?"

"It was Hillman's son Colin who told me about Jillian. He showed up outside my apartment and told me about her. He works on his dad's campaign, and he said they had received a tip about her."

"You have his number?" Rod asked. "I'd like to talk to him."

"Don't waste your time," Sage said. "He already told me he would deny everything."

"Wow," Rod said, and there was some more of that head shaking.

"You have to understand the man has it in for me," Sage said. "He wanted me to track down that girl. He might have even been the one chasing us in that silver Prius. I wouldn't put it past him."

"I want to help you, I do," Rod said, "but I just don't know anymore. I feel like maybe I'm not doing you any favors. I mean, abducting a minor, you realize that's some serious shit, right? They'll send you away for that."

"Come on," Sage said. "You know me. You know I wouldn't do something like that."

"Yeah," Rod agreed. "The old you wouldn't have, but I don't know anymore."

"What? You think I got stressed out because I lost my job and my mother's in the hospital, and now I'm running around kidnapping teenage girls?"

"They searched your car," Rod said quietly.

"What's that supposed to mean?"

Rod sucked in a big mouthful of air. "They found your empties."

"Empties?" Sage said.

"Look, I know you started drinking again," Rod said. "Frankly, it's sort of a relief. It explains why you've been behaving so erratically."

Then Sage remembered the bottles he found in his recycling bin. The one's he had been taking to Giselle to have her analyze at the lab. He had never taken them out of his car.

"It's not what you think," Sage said. "Those aren't mine."

"Look, even my gullible parents didn't buy the I'm-holding-it-for-a-friend excuse when I was fifteen and they found a bag of weed in my bedroom."

"No, really," Sage said. "I found them in my recycling bin."

"Then what were they doing in your car?"

Sage was about to explain that he had been taking them for analysis, that he knew a woman who worked in a DNA testing lab, but he stopped himself. Explaining that he was taking empty liquor bottles to a woman who had just been murdered wasn't going to help his defense any.

"I don't know where they came from," Sage admitted.

"You need help," Rod said. "Do you promise to get help? Go to a clinic, go to a meeting, whatever works for you?"

"I'm not an alcoholic," Sage said. But Rod knew Sage was the guy who ordered diet soda when they went out to the bar. Of course he assumed Sage had a drinking problem.

"I need you to promise me," Rod said. "If you promise me, I'll talk to them, fight for you, explain it was all a big misunderstanding. No guarantees, but I think I can talk them out of charging you, but you have to promise me."

"Okay, yes, I promise," Sage said.

"You mean it? You'll get help?"

Sage nodded. "Yes," he said quietly. His friend did have a point. He definitely needed help. He just didn't think he was going to find it at an Alcoholics Anonymous meeting.

The bag of empty alcohol bottles was missing from his car, along with every discarded chip bag and scrap of paper that had cluttered the floor. He supposed he should be grateful for the clean out. Mostly he was grateful that somehow Rod had managed to talk Rayanne out of charging him. The small-town police force had a tendency to look out for their own, but Sage was pleasantly surprised that the favor even extended to former members.

As he sat in his car still parked in the station's lot, he

thought about what he had promised Rod. He had never in his life gone to an Alcoholics Anonymous meeting, let alone a rehab facility. Did he even belong at either of those places?

It was true that in college he drank too much, but if every college kid who over-indulged in alcohol could be labeled an alcoholic, well, the country was in trouble. But Sage was also familiar with the warning signs of alcoholism. Drinking to the point of blacking out was on there. Being in denial about having a drinking problem was another. What if without realizing it he was a recovering alcoholic?

Melodie's death had scared him sober. Some people needed a twelve-step program, some a stay in rehab. All he had needed was for his sister to be viciously murdered.

But real alcoholics couldn't be scared into sobriety, could they? Maybe the best thing to do would be to talk to someone, a counselor of some sort. He knew that was what he should do, but he felt like he couldn't do that until he had all the facts. And right now, the fact that he needed to know the most was where those empty bottles had come from.

He needed to have them tested. They had been rinsed out, but there could still be DNA traces, he reasoned. Had they been logged as evidence? If not, they might have simply been tossed. There was a dumpster behind the station. It was worth a shot.

Sage was halfway in the dumpster when someone called his name. He pulled his head out of the smelly bin and turned around, only to see Rayanne, his former boss, the chief of the Culver Creek Police Department, standing in a pool of artificial light and regarding him with concern.

"You lose something?" she asked.

"Do you know where the stuff removed from my car went?" he asked.

"Chet should have returned all your possessions," she said.

Sage had gotten his phone, keys and wallet, as well as a tire gauge, half a bottle of hand sanitizer and a single winter glove that he didn't remember ever seeing before from the officer manning the intake desk, but the bag with the empty bottles had not been included.

"There was a bag with some empty bottles in it," Sage said.

"We have to log any items that are confiscated officially," Rayanne said. "They become part of public record."

"Are they being held for evidence?" Sage asked. "They need to be DNA tested."

"I don't think you're hearing me." Her voice was firm. "We have to log any confiscated items officially."

"Yeah, you said that, but . . ." His words trailed off as he realized what Rayanne was saying. They had erased the existence of the empty alcohol bottles in his car. They had not been logged as possessions. They had not been entered into evidence. It was to protect him, maybe even to protect their own asses as well. "There's not any chance I could get them?"

"Maybe it would be best to let this go," Rayanne suggested.

She turned and started to walk in the direction of her pickup, but she stopped suddenly and turned to face him.

"I had my concerns about hiring you," she said. The remark puzzled Sage. His work record had been spotless. "I mean because of the other stuff. That unpleasantness with your sister."

It had been a long and draining day, and it took every ounce of effort for Sage not to snap at his former boss for referring to his sister's murder as "that unpleasantness."

"I don't see what that has to do with anything," he said.

"I like to do my homework," Rayanne said. She paused, and Sage was about to walk away, when she said. "I remember some people thought you had killed her. The timeline all worked out, as I recall."

But Sage had never been under official police investigation for his sister's death. The only people who thought he killed Melodie were users on the web sleuth forum.

"You read the forums?" Sage asked. She wasn't kidding when she said she did her homework.

"Not when I was hiring you," she was quick to point out. "Back in the day I was with the state police, and I monitored various websites, social media sites."

Unlike Rayanne, Sage hadn't done his homework, and he was surprised to learn she wasn't a lifer with the Culver Creek Police Department.

"Hanging out on Facebook hardly sounds like exciting police work," he said.

She shrugged. "You would be surprised how many criminals get caught because they post something incriminating online. Those web sleuth forums are crawling with thugs. It draws them in like a moth to a flame. They should be grateful they've managed to elude the authorities, but it's like they can't help themselves."

"I wouldn't presume to understand the mindset of a murderer," Sage said.

"No, of course not," she said. "But you were active on the forums, weren't you? That's what drew you here, wasn't it? The Lily Esposito cold case?"

Sage thought back to the day someone had shared the job posting about the detective job opening in Culver Creek. In his mind, it was one of the forum regulars. He stared down at the dark ground as he tried to picture the posting that was shared with him. He couldn't remember who it was. Someone who knew Sage had gone into law enforcement, definitely. There were only a handful of forum users who he had shared private messages with. PhillyFury aka Ambrose Radcliffe, had been one, but Sage didn't think that was who shared the job posting with him.

"Was it—" Sage started to ask, but when he looked up, he saw that Rayanne had walked back to her truck, and a few seconds later, her taillights came on and she backed out of the parking spot and left the lot.

She thought he was a criminal. No formal accusation had been made, but he hadn't missed her suggestion.

37

SAGE JUMPED when he opened the door of his apartment and saw Zoey Wilson sitting on his couch.

"Thank God," she said.

"What are you doing here?" He glanced at the doorjamb for evidence that she had forced the door open.

"Your landlord let me in," Zoey said. "I told him I was worried. No one had seen you in days, and the last phone message you left for me was troubling. We thought you might be dead in here."

It seemed like a complete overreaction, but he reminded himself that not very long ago Zoey's boyfriend had been murdered, something she only learned when she called his cell phone after he had not returned home the previous evening. He supposed that could make someone a little bit touchy.

"Still alive," he muttered. He walked past her on the couch and went into the kitchen. The first thing he did was check his recycling bin. It did not appear that any more empty alcohol bottles had been added to it.

"What are you doing?" She had gotten up and now stood in the doorway to the kitchen.

He didn't like the way she was looking at him. The almost pitying look reminded him of how Rayanne looked a few minutes ago in the station parking lot.

"Just checking to see if you had added anything," he said in a clipped, angry tone.

"I don't know what that means," she said, "but speaking of things I don't understand, would you care to explain that voice-mail message?"

"What message?" He had the sudden compulsion to check the rest of the apartment. Maybe she had added something to his bathroom trash bin or put something in the drawer of his dresser.

She followed close on his heels and stood watching him as he ransacked his own apartment. He looked up when he heard a tinny voice from a cell phone speaker. It took him a moment to recognize it as his own.

"Listen, if you could do me a favor and just say, if anyone asks, that I was with you tonight."

And now he remembered calling Zoey and leaving that message. He had just left Giselle's apartment building. He had been in a panicked state as he raced to get back home. The call was a stupid idea born out of his fear and his exhausted mind.

"Never mind about that," Sage said.

"Where were you?" she asked. "What's going on?"

If Zoey told any of this to the police, after what happened this afternoon, it would not look good at all.

"It was nothing. I was just overtired," he said. "And speaking of which, I'm feeling kind of beat right now." He was exhausted but way too keyed up to even think about sleeping. He didn't think Zoey could tell.

"Can you just tell me what's going on?"

"I found out who the other half sibling was, the other one who was murdered," Sage explained. "His name was Justin Turner."

"The psychic's son?" Zoey asked.

"You knew him?" Sage asked.

"Not really." Zoey turned and walked away from him, back into the living room, where she grabbed her purse and her jacket like she was about to leave.

Sage grabbed hold of her shoulder to stop her, and loosed his grip when he felt her flinch.

"How do you know Justin Turner?"

She shook her head. Her face had turned pink.

"I need to know what you know," he said.

She stepped away from him toward the door. Who could blame her? He sounded like a police detective trying to intimidate a suspect.

"So, when I was in high school, I became obsessed with the idea of psychics," Zoey said. "I don't know, I guess I figured they were in touch with the spiritual realm, ghosts and all that."

It took tremendous willpower not to scoff at her or roll his eyes or something. He shouldn't have been surprised that a woman who used to focus on selling only haunted houses or houses she claimed were haunted would have also been the sort of teenager to spend her money on psychics, but he was disgusted with the idea. His own mother had for a time been forking money over to some psychic charlatan.

"I can't believe you wasted your money on some fake like that," Sage said.

"Yeah, yeah, I know," Zoey said, "but Madame Turner wasn't fake. She really was psychic."

"Come on," he said. "You're smarter than that."

"She knew there was going to be a bomb scare at my high school," Zoey said.

"She probably called it in."

"She knew I wouldn't graduate college," Zoey said. "I mean, she told me that before I even started college."

"Planted the idea in your head is more like it," Sage said.

Zoey edged closer to the door, and when she spoke again her voice was quiet and edged with fear. "She told me a man in my life was not going to be who I thought he was. I have to go."

She opened the door and stepped out into the hall. He knew he should let her go, that it wouldn't help his case any if he went after her, but he didn't always do what he knew was the right thing.

"Don't you think she might have been talking about your father?" Sage said as he followed her out into the hall. She was already at the other end of it, about to head down the stairs. "I mean, you thought he was a murderer, but then it turned out he hadn't killed that girl, after all."

Zoey didn't respond. She started down the stairs.

So in a louder voice Sage said, "And what about your boyfriend? Kiefer was running some real estate scam using your name!"

"Shut up!" he heard someone yell from inside one of the other apartments.

Sage felt like he had no choice but to follow her down the stairs. He left his door ajar and ran after her.

When he caught up with her outside on the sidewalk, she turned to look at him and there were tears in her eyes. He hadn't expected that.

"Justin wasn't murdered," she said.

"It was never announced in the papers," he explained, "because the police weren't able to identify his body."

"No," Zoey said, "I saw him the other day. In the coffee shop parking lot."

Had she been seeing ghosts again? Like when she saw

Melodie after her own sister tried to kill her? He almost said something to this effect, but he remembered something else— Briggs at the Pleasant Oaks police station saying the man he had beat up was Justin Turner.

"What coffee shop?" Sage demanded as a feeling of agitation assailed him.

"What?"

"It was Pleasant Perk, wasn't it?"

"Yeah, I think so," Zoey said. "But what does that have to with anything?"

But he barely heard her as he ran to his car.

38

LENNIE WAS WAITING for Justin at his desk when he walked in. That wasn't unusual, but there was a dark look in Lennie's eyes that worried Justin.

For his part, Justin was sore and exhausted. Sleeping in his car had been no picnic.

"I think you know what I'm doing here," Lennie said.

"I'm not sure," Justin said.

"You know, I thought it was weird when you showed up here looking like you had gone five rounds with a prizefighter, but I let it slide because on the phone no one can see your bruises, right?"

Justin nodded. He was still standing behind his desk chair, not sure whether he should sit down or not.

"But you must know, as part of your agreement to work here, I get any reports on criminal activity you're involved in, right?" Lennie asked.

He figured it had to be good old Brick Dick. It was hardly fair. He hadn't done anything wrong.

"I was framed," Justin said, "by a corrupt cop."

"How does someone get framed for getting the shit kicked out of them?" Lennie asked. "Look, I saw your face. There's no point lying about it."

"Oh." Justin was confused. "I'm in trouble for getting beat up?"

"Nice try," his boss said, "but old Lennie isn't the idiot you think he is. In fact, on a certain internet forum, they consider me an ace detective."

"You're a PI?" Justin was growing nervous and tried not to let it show. He gripped his seat back to keep his hand from trembling.

"I could be," Lennie said, "but I like a steady paycheck, even if it means working at this hellhole."

This earned a few chuckles from some of Justin's fellow call center workers. Lennie was usually Mr. Positivity and never dared to denigrate the psychic sweatshop he managed.

"The thing is, Virgil, what you might not realize is that as part of my duties I have to reconcile all orders that our new hires receive. Make sure everything's on the up and up. The other thing you might not realize is that I have a near photographic memory."

And now Justin understood what the problem was.

"So, when I see that address on the police report, a little light bulb went off in my head," Lennie said. "Because I had definitely seen that address before, so I go look up your orders, and sure enough, there it is, a few days before, you had received an order from a Kelly Dorian at that address. That gets me thinking, and so I Google the name Kelly Dorian, and lo and behold—"

But Justin didn't wait to hear the rest. He turned and ran. His feet had never flown so fast as he sprinted through the maze of cubicles, down the stairs, and burst out the front door. His hands shook like mad as he tried to unlock his door, and he wasted precious seconds. But he got the thing unlocked and got inside before anyone came after him.

He tore out of the parking lot, determined to get as far away as he possibly could. California. That seemed like far enough away. But getting to California was going to take an awful lot of gas, and a whole lot of money. And just the thought of being a broke, scared guy living out of his car brought back some bad memories.

After three nights of sleeping in his car, Justin had developed a sore throat and a bad cough. The nights were too cold, and he wasn't getting enough to eat. He couldn't live on stuff he raided out of dumpsters forever. In fact, he was pretty sure he couldn't do it for one more night.

Did he dare to go home? Maybe the murderer had given up by now. He could at least drive by the place and see if anything looked amiss, but just thinking about that made him tremble with fear, or maybe those were chills from the fever he now had. He wasn't sure. Either way, he decided it was too risky to go back to the house.

But there was somewhere he could go to. He knew from his research where Virgil Chandler lived, and he knew from their conversation that Virgil lived alone. What if the murderer was at Virgil's place waiting for him? No, the murderer didn't know where Virgil lived. The murderer didn't even know Virgil's name. And it was then, as he drove in a feverish state with a growling stomach, that Justin came up with his plan.

This whole mess he was in was because Virgil Chandler

had stolen Justin's identity. The only solution that made sense in Justin's fevered mind to make things right was to steal Virgil's identity. He was no longer Justin Turner. Justin Turner had been murdered. Henceforth he would be Virgil Chandler.

39

"YOU WANT me to tell you exactly what happened on a night more than six years ago?" Frances asked. It was nearly closing time at Pleasant Perk, and Melodie's former coworker was busy tidying the place up. She was clearly annoyed with Sage's barrage of questions, but he didn't care. He needed to know the truth.

"You said before that you saw me here that night," Sage said. "You said something about me waiting in the parking lot for her."

"I don't know," she said. "I mean, I guess I was wrong. That must have been another night."

"No, you said last time that I was here that night."

"Look, it was six years ago, okay?" She sounded annoyed. "I might be confusing things. You used to come meet her here sometimes."

It was true. When he had been home from college on break, he would show up at the coffee shop a few minutes before it closed. Sometimes it was because Melodie's car was on the fritz again, and he was giving her a ride home, but other times the two of them were headed to a late movie or going to that twenty-four-hour pancake place down the road. So sure, Frances could have been thinking of one of those nights, but before when he had spoken to her, she specifically said he was there the night Melodie was killed.

"But I didn't come in here, right?" Sage said. "You said I was just out in the parking lot."

"Yeah, that's right. It was just me and her walking out to our cars, and I could see you in your car at the far side of the lot. You know, it's weird, but I don't remember Melodie going over to you and saying hi or anything. I mean, maybe she texted you or something. I think she was looking down at her phone."

"Maybe," Sage said. But of course, he knew Melodie hadn't texted him, and he had no recollection of ever meeting Melodie here and just hanging out in the parking lot. He had loved coffee back in those days, and if he got here close enough to closing, she wouldn't bother to charge him for coffee that was about to get dumped anyway. "Do you remember if she said anything or acknowledged me in some way? Waved or something?"

Frances stopped what she was doing and frowned. "No. That's strange, isn't it? Maybe she just didn't see you there. But like I said, I might just have my nights wrong. It was a long time ago."

The coffee shop was deserted at this hour. The place shouldn't even have been in business anymore after Sage tipped off the state police about the illegal prostitution ring being run from the premises, but the investigation appeared to be moving forward at a snail's pace. Sage couldn't help but wonder if that pace was in part due to the fact that some local bigwigs had been customers of Pleasant Perk's side business over the years. Blackmail could be a pretty powerful motivator. Was that also why his sister's murderer had never been caught?

"What about the lighting? Did you get new parking lot lights since then?"

"Same lights," she said.

"So you could see me clearly?" he asked. "You're sure it was me."

"I'm not sure of anything," she admitted. "But yeah, I mean, it looked like you and your car. So I guess I just figured it was you."

"If it walks like a duck, and talks like a duck," Sage muttered.

"What?"

"Nothing."

"So, I'm done here, unless you want to ask me what the weather was like six years ago or what I ate for breakfast that morning or something else I won't be able to answer with any degree of accuracy."

"No, that's all for now," Sage said.

Would Frances really have mistaken Justin for Sage. They were roughly the same height, but otherwise they didn't look much alike, and it wasn't like you could tell how tall someone was when they were sitting in their car. And that was the other thing. Back in college, Sage drove an old Toyota Supra that broke down roughly every other week. The thing was, even at night it would be hard to mistake Justin's Subaru wagon for a Supra. Then again, six years ago, maybe Justin had been driving something else, maybe something more Supra-looking. Sage was so lost in thought as he exited the coffee shop, he paid no attention to the man on his way in, but the other customer saw Sage.

"Hey!" he shouted, and Sage looked up to see Colin Hillman walking in.

Fate was a peculiar thing.

"Well, well," Sage said, "this is a nice bit of luck."

"Hey, can I buy you a coffee?" Colin asked, and Sage could not believe the way this spoiled rich boy was grinning like his smile and a hot beverage could make everything all right.

"You can go screw yourself," Sage said, and if he hadn't just been released by the police a few hours ago, he might not have been able to resist the urge to take a swing at Colin's smug, pretty boy face. But this was Pleasant Oaks, and the Hillmans were basically the local deities.

Colin held up his hands and made a face like Sage was overreacting.

"Come off your high horse," Sage said. "I know what the hell that stunt of yours was about this morning. Your father put you up to that? Or did you come up with that idea all on your own?"

"Uh, I'm not sure what you're talking about," Colin said.

The two men stood just outside the coffee shop, and when Sage glanced inside, he could see Frances watching him. It felt like she was silently judging him, but maybe that was just his paranoia flaring up.

"That hot tip you decided to give me this morning?" Sage said. "Pretty convenient that the girl was right in Culver Creek. Too bad she isn't in any way related to your father."

"Crap," Colin said. "That's my fault. We should have vetted it first. I mean, we get all kinds of BS that comes in, but after what we were talking about . . ." Colin paused to look around as if he was worried someone might be listening, but the coffee shop parking lot was deserted. "I guess I was just worried that the girl might be in trouble."

Again Sage had to fight the urge to strike Colin Hillman.

"I could have gone to jail!" Sage roared.

Colin looked puzzled, and as Sage considered what had happened earlier today, he realized he couldn't place all the blame on Colin Hillman. Was it possible the senator's only legitimate son had deliberately tried to set him up? Absolutely, and Sage had no reason to absolve him of that crime just yet, but Sage should have done his own homework before assuming Jillian was his half sister. Certainly, he shouldn't have dragged the girl into his car without first determining who she was and verifying she was in danger.

Looking back on the way he behaved this afternoon, he saw what Rod had seen—a man who was spiraling out of control at a frightening rate. It scared him.

"Hey, are you okay?" Colin asked, and Sage saw genuine concern in the other man's eyes, but he still wasn't sure if he trusted him.

"Yeah, fine," Sage said. "Just tired. It's been a long day."

Sage headed toward his car. He felt Colin's eyes on him, and it wasn't until Sage reached the vehicle that he finally heard the door to the coffee shop swing open. He glanced back and saw Colin head inside. That was when it occurred to him that it was awfully late to be making a coffee run.

Sage waited until he saw the lights go off inside Pleasant Perk before he jumped out of his car, one of only two still left in the coffee shop's lot. As he trotted across the parking lot he was reminded of those times he had met Melodie here at the end of her shift, and what he would have given to see his sister there walking alongside Frances, exhausted but still smiling. He missed her smile so much.

"Oh!" Frances said, and she made a little noise like a small animal. Her eyes darted about, as if looking for someone to save her from the creepy guy in the parking lot, and he took a step backward to give her more space. He didn't want to repeat the same mistake he had made earlier with Jillian.

"Is Colin a regular?" Sage asked.

"Who's Colin?" she asked.

"The last guy who was in there—chiseled jaw, million-watt smile, cocky attitude."

She smiled. "Oh, you mean Virgil. Virgil Chandler." She laughed at this.

"Was he here for coffee?"

"Most men don't use an alias to buy coffee, do they?" she asked, which proved she knew damn well who he was. She laughed again.

"What's so funny?" he asked.

"It's just that back in the day, his father was a regular here, and let's just say he wasn't a big coffee drinker."

Sage felt suddenly sick to his stomach.

"When Melodie worked here," he said.

"Oh, no, way before that. I think he stopped coming once he got into politics. Too risky. But the thing is, the girl he had a thing for, her name was Chandler. Bianca Chandler. Kind of freaky, isn't it, that his son picked the name Chandler as an alias?"

"Yeah," Sage agreed. "Freaky." Too freaky, in his opinion.

40

BIANCA CHANDLER DIED of a drug overdose at just twenty-seven years of age, nearly twenty years ago. Sage stared at the digitized death notice on his computer screen. It was the last sentence that chilled Sage to the bone. Bianca was survived by her young son, Virgil.

Sage figured the odds that Colin Hillman had just randomly picked the name Virgil Chandler as an alias were about a million to one, which meant Colin was a liar at best and a sociopathic murderer at worst. Because if Colin knew about Virgil Chandler, then he knew about Melodie as well. It was no coincidence that Colin and Melodie had been dating. Colin probably hunted her down, and now he was toying with Sage like a cat with a mouse.

The third result down when Sage Googled Virgil Chandler's name was a news article about the man being arrested for passing bad checks a little over seven years ago. But it was what Frances would have dubbed a "freaky" coincidence that caught his eye. The officer who collared Virgil Chandler was with the state police's fraud division, and her name was Rayanne Lawrence.

~

A s he turned down Rayanne's road, a brief burst of rationality told him it was way too late to be showing up unannounced at anyone's house, let alone the home of the Culver Creek chief of police, the woman who had fired him. He fully intended to turn around and return home, wait until the morning or maybe until Monday morning when he could contact her at the station, but as he drove past her house, he saw lights on in multiple windows and he counted four cars in her driveway. One was Rayanne's truck, and the silver sedan beside it probably belonged to her husband, but the two parked behind them must be guests.

He figured it was safe to assume he wouldn't be waking Rayanne up, but did he want to interrupt her social gathering, or should he just stick to his revised plan and get ahold of her in the morning? In his mind he could see his sister glaring at him. He had tried to put off talking to her when what she needed more than anything in the world was her brother to be there for her. Putting off important conversations could be dangerous. Sometimes people wound up dead.

Rayanne looked surprised, and maybe just a bit nervous, when she opened up her front door.

"Sage," she said. "What are you doing here?"

"I need to talk to you," he said.

"Could this wait, perhaps?" she asked. "Some of my husband's friends from work are over right now."

"I need to ask you about Virgil Chandler," Sage said. He saw something, a sort of flicker in her eyes was how he would describe it, and then it was gone.

"Who's Virgil Chandler?" she asked.

"You arrested him," he said. "About seven years ago."

"That's when I was with the state police," she said.

"Right," he said. "According to the newspaper article, he was writing bad checks."

"Yeah, I saw a lot of that back then," she said. "But his name doesn't stand out."

She was lying. Sage was sure of it.

"I'd like to talk to him," Sage said. "Do you know where he wound up?"

"Prison would be my guess," she said. "Sorry I can't be of much help, but I need to get back."

She was seconds away from politely but firmly shutting the door in his face.

"How long did you work for the state police? I guess I always figured you were a lifetime Culver Creek cop, maybe followed in your dad's footsteps or something."

Rayanne made a face at him, but at least she wasn't trying to shut the door.

"My father wasn't a cop." She narrowed her eyes at Sage. "What are you really doing here?"

"As far as the internet's concerned, you're the last person to have contact with Virgil Chandler."

She laughed at this, a high-pitched, girly-sounding laugh that didn't sound much like the Rayanne he knew. He suspected she might be a little drunk, but that was what he got for showing up unannounced at her house on a Friday night.

"Look, you're probably not going to find him under that name," Rayanne said.

"Why's that?"

"When I brought him in, the guy had like five different driver's licenses on him," she said. "Honestly, I'm not even sure Virgil Chandler is his real name."

Like Colin, Sage thought, and he wondered what the odds were on two different guys picking the same unlikely alias.

"A few seconds ago, you didn't remember him at all," Sage reminded her.

"And a few seconds before that, I was enjoying a quiet evening with friends before some loose cannon former employee showed up at my front door," she said.

Well, she had him there. He gave her a little sheepish shrug. Somewhere along the line, he had gone from respected detective to loose cannon. His parents had been disappointed with him when he chose a career in law enforcement. Maybe they had realized it wouldn't work out.

"Did old Mr. Lawrence approve of you becoming a cop?" Sage asked.

"My father-in-law?" Rayanne asked.

Of course, Lawrence would be her married name. That was the whole problem with Colin's list. So few of those women had held on to their maiden names. Tracking them down was next to impossible.

"Well, Mr. . . . ." Sage waved his hand in the air, in place of guessing at Rayanne's maiden name.

"Everett," she supplied. "But actually, that was my mother's name. My father didn't stick around."

"She must be proud of you," Sage said, trying to make up for his earlier gaffe but feeling like he was floundering in water way over his head.

"Look, much as I'd love to stand here all night discussing my family history, I think I better get back to my guests."

"Of course," Sage said. "Sorry."

He had wasted his time coming here. All he succeeded in doing was annoying Rayanne and embarrassing himself.

He waved goodbye and started back down the walk toward the driveway.

"I hope you have some luck finding Justin!" she called after him.

That stopped him short. He hadn't told Rayanne anything about Justin. But the police report must be a matter of public record. Maybe as her former employee she had received a copy automatically.

"Justin?" Sage asked.

"Wait, what was his name?" she asked. "No, it was Virgil, wasn't it? Virgil Chandler. Like I said, he had a few aliases."

41

AFTER DRIVING around the block three times, Justin pulled into the parking lot of his apartment complex. He didn't see any cop cars around, but that didn't mean anything. They could be using an unmarked vehicle.

He shouldn't have come back here, but he didn't know what else to do. What he needed more than anything else in the world right now was a warm bed. Sleeping in your car several nights in a row turned out to not be so good for your health. Justin had come down with a cold, and what started out as minor irritation had blossomed into a full-on, sniffling, coughing, bone-aching illness. If he wasn't feeling so miserable and so desperate, he would have tried to stick it out a few more nights, but the truth was, he wasn't good at being a criminal, he never had been.

He thought of that day six years ago, when he had shown up at the address he had for Virgil, a different crappy apartment but not all that much different than this one. Justin had attempted to break in, first through the front door and then through a sliding glass door. It had taken him hours, and in the end, he ended up heaving a brick through the sliding door, sure that the sound of shattering glass would bring the neighbors running and that he would be hauled off to jail for breaking and entering. But in that neighborhood, nobody batted an eye at the loud crash.

As lousy as he was at breaking into apartments, he was even worse at assuming someone else's identity. For more than a month he skulked about the place, wearing hats and sunglasses anytime he needed to step out his door, practically running anytime he saw one of the neighbors about. Each night he tossed and turned in bed, sure the police would break down the door and haul him away or some friend or relative would come looking for Virgil and freak out when they found a strange man squatting in his apartment.

So he made it a priority to save up as much money as he could so he could move out of this place. That task proved more challenging than he expected. It was surprisingly simple to become Virgil Chandler officially. He wasn't surprised that Virgil had stolen his identity when he saw how easy it was to get a driver's license with his own photo and the other man's name on it.

What proved to be difficult was getting a job with the name Virgil Chandler. It turned out that Virgil's checkered past meant a lot of employers wouldn't even consider hiring him. Virgil had a police record and a spotty work history, and Justin was stuck making do with the lousiest jobs out there.

In those first few weeks of living life as Virgil Chandler, Justin had some deep misgivings and a strong desire to return to his old life. Becoming Virgil made him realize just how good he'd had it before.

He should have listened to Officer Briggs. He never should have gone looking for the man who had stolen his identity. What would happen if he went back to his old life? But he knew deep down that he could never do that. The murderer was out there waiting for him, maybe the police too. He had no desire to live in fear, he'd done enough of that already. But some nights, tossing and turning in Virgil Chandler's bed, Justin wondered if it really mattered if he was spending his sleepless nights as another man or if he was spending them back home where he belonged.

But by the time he saved up enough money to move out of Virgil's apartment, the latter option was off the table. His old house had gone into foreclosure. He saw the sign out front one afternoon when he drove past the place with tears streaming down his face. It was like Justin Turner had been fully erased from existence.

So now when a sneezing and sniffling man, who had more or less become the man who had destroyed his life, pulled the mail that had piled up out of his box, he felt a small flurry of excitement when he saw the envelope from Human History. Justin Turner had not been fully erased from the world, and maybe somewhere out there he had relatives he had never met. Probably he could never meet up with them, not without risking everything, but just the thought that there might be someone out there filled him with hope.

42

SAGE AWOKE TO A POUNDING SOUND. He lifted his head up and winced. He had fallen asleep sitting up at his dining room table, his head using the pile of papers spread out on it for a pillow. His body was not at all happy with his choice of a bed. The pounding sound was coming from his front door.

With stiff, aching muscles he got up and shuffled over to the door. When he opened it, Rod was standing there carrying two to-go cups on a cardboard tray and a grease-stained paper bag.

"I brought breakfast," Rod announced as he stepped past Sage into the apartment. "I see you've been hard at work cleaning the place." This latter bit was clearly sarcasm.

"Did I forget about something? Was this some appointment I don't remember making?" Sage asked. He rubbed at his face, where a few days' worth of stubble had accumulated.

"I figured if I gave you too much advance warning you would figure out some way to blow me off," Rod said. "I hope you like egg sandwiches."

Rod had already cleared some room at the table and was unpacking two foil-wrapped breakfast sandwiches. Sage's mouth watered as he caught a glimpse of a kaiser roll thick with a mound of eggs and cheese that had gone all melty and gooey.

"You really don't know me at all if you think I would blow off that sandwich," Sage said as he sat down at the table.

Rod slid one of the to-go cups to him, and peering into it, Sage was pleased to see it was a cup of green tea. Well, it looked like Rod did know him pretty well.

"Yeah, the sandwich wasn't what I was worried you would blow off," Rod said.

"You're buttering me up for something," Sage surmised when he swallowed down an oversized bite of artery-clogging deliciousness.

"I want you to go to a meeting with me," Rod said. "I figured it's the kind of thing where it might be helpful to have a friend along."

"I'm guessing this isn't a meeting of the local chapter of out-of-work police officers," Sage said.

"An AA meeting, meets at a church on the other end of town," Rod said.

If Sage wasn't so hungry, and the sandwich didn't taste so good, Sage might have walked away from the table, but instead he sat silently chewing, though his breakfast didn't taste nearly so good now that he had learned the purpose of his friend's visit.

"What's this all about?" Rod said, holding up a piece of paper. "Who are all these women?"

It was the list from Colin. Sage had been working on that some more before he fell asleep. After what Rayanne had said, he had the brilliant idea to try to track down the married names of the women on the list, but he hadn't been having much success.

"It has to do with my sister's case," Sage said.

"I hope you're not planning on abducting any of them," Rod said. He laughed to indicate he was joking, but Sage could see that Rod was concerned.

"It's nothing like that," Sage said.

"Yeah, it just seems a little creepy," Rod said. "I'm just worried this whole thing is really unhealthy."

Sage wasn't about to argue with his friend. He thought Rod might have a point. Things had started to feel overwhelming, and there was ample evidence that he was not doing such a good job of keeping things together. But he wasn't an alcoholic, and there was no need for him to go to an AA meeting.

"I appreciate that you want to help me," Sage said. "God knows, I certainly didn't do anything to deserve your friendship—"

"Once a coworker, always a friend," Rod quipped.

"Yeah, but I don't have a drinking problem, and I don't need—"

Sage stopped. Rod's words had finally penetrated his brain. He thought of what Rayanne said last night when he had showed up at her house. Her husband's friends from work were over. When you were a kid, your friends were the people you went to school with, but when you were an adult, you often became friends with the people you worked with. All those women on the list from Colin Hillman had worked at the same law firm his mother had. Maybe they hadn't all been there at the same time, but some of them probably were, and some of them would have been friends with her.

"I need to go to the hospital." Sage had devoured his whole breakfast sandwich and about a third of his cup of tea. "I have to talk to my mother."

"She woke up from the coma?" Rod asked, excited. "That's great news!"

Sage shook his head.

"No, not yet," he said, and he realized the futility in his plan, but no, his dad would be there, and his dad knew his mother when she worked at the law firm. He would probably know which of the women on Colin's list had been his mom's friends. Maybe they stayed in touch. Maybe he knew how to contact them. "My father, though. I can talk to him."

"That's great," Rod said. "We can swing by that meeting first, and then you can head over to the hospital."

"I'm not an alcoholic," Sage assured him.

Rod gave him a disappointed look.

"What?" Sage said. "I'm not."

"Rayanne called me," Rod said. "She told me about last night."

"Last night?" Sage said. Clearly it had been a mistake for him to show up at her house. He realized that now, but it was nothing but a little lapse in judgment.

"She told me how you showed up there staggering drunk, ranting and raving. Look, you don't have to be embarrassed about falling off the wagon. It happens to everyone."

"I wasn't ever on any wagon to fall off of!" Sage shouted. The rage was boiling up in him again, and it caused him to jump out of his seat. If he was trying to prove to Rod that he had everything under control, he was doing a terrible job. "And I was completely sober last night when I went to Rayanne's house. I had a question about some old case she was on, and it was a mistake to go there, but—"

"Then where's your car?" Rod demanded.

"What?" Sage was suddenly relieved. This was an argument he would win easily. "It's parked outside."

He went over to the front window and pointed at the spot across the road where he had parked last night. Only it wasn't his car parked there. Wait, was that the spot he had parked in last night? He might be mixing up his days. Clearly, he must have parked in another spot last night. He scanned up and down the road, pressing his forehead up against the cool glass in an effort to track down his car.

"It's at Rayanne's," Rod said. "She told me you were too drunk to drive, so she drove you back here."

"No," Sage said, shaking his head. He hadn't been drunk, and he had driven himself home from Rayanne's house, but now as he tried to replay the events of the previous evening, he couldn't actually remember the drive home, or parking his car, or even coming back inside his apartment. He was sure he had done all these things, but he had only a hazy memory, and the truth was, he wasn't sure if these memories were from another night or not. "My car's at Rayanne's?"

"She said you left it in front of her house," Rod said.

If his car was at Rayanne's, then that seemed to prove he had in fact shown up there drunk, but he didn't have a single memory of this, and what's more, he did have a memory of being there in a completely sober state. Was his memory a lie? The disorientation and confusion were very unsettling.

"We'll swing by there after the meeting." Rod stood up now too, and he started to gather their trash in the grease-stained bag. "I'm going to hit the john first before we head to that meeting."

Sage tried to mask his relief and nodded. He tried to act casual while Rod took a seeming eternity to clean up and dump the trash. When finally his friend closed the bathroom door behind him, Sage grabbed Colin's list and his phone and moved as quietly as he could out of his apartment.

S age had switched his cell phone to silent during the long Uber ride from Culver Creek to Pleasant Oaks because Rod had been calling and texting him repeatedly. He knew he had to call his friend back. Rod deserved that much, but first Sage needed to talk to his father.

Sage found him camped out in his usual spot in his mother's hospital room. His mother looked unchanged.

"How is she?" Sage asked.

His father shrugged. "No changes. How are you doing?"

He could tell by his father's tone that he probably looked like crap. Maybe he should have at least glanced in a mirror before making his getaway. He needed a shower and a shave. A decent night's sleep in an actual bed probably would help, too. Soon, he promised himself.

"I've been better," Sage said. "I have a favor to ask you, though. I have a list of women who worked at the law firm Mom did. I wondered if you could look at it, see if you recognize any of the names."

"Why are you doing this?" his dad asked, and Sage was reminded of Rod saying he was worried that Sage's obsession with this case was unhealthy.

"It's something I need to do," Sage said. He tried not to think about the fact that he couldn't remember the previous night, that he had likely embarrassed himself forever by showing up drunk at his former boss's home. "Please can you just take a look?"

Sage took the paper out of his pocket and unfolded it. His father shrugged and held out his hand. Sage passed it over.

"Did Mom stay in touch with any of the women she used to work with? Were any of them close friends?"

"At the law firm?" his father asked. "No, I think she really wanted to do everything she could to forget she had ever worked at that awful place."

Which apparently was why she couldn't even bring herself to tell her children the truth about who their real father was.

His father studied the list, but after a minute or so he shook his head.

"Sorry," his dad said, "I don't recognize any of the names."

Sage wasn't surprised. After all, the list had come from Colin Hillman, and considering the other tip he had received from Colin, the one that turned out to be a total lie, Sage didn't have a lot of faith in this list. For all he knew, none of these women had ever worked at the law firm. The only woman he was confident had been involved with Mick Hillman and maybe had one of his children was Bianca Chandler. But that wasn't a name he had gotten from Colin, well, not directly anyway.

Why did Colin use the name Virgil Chandler as an alias? If he wanted to fly below the radar, wouldn't it make sense to use a less conspicuous name like Joe Anderson or Mike Smith? Why Virgil Chandler?

"There's someone you could talk to," his dad said, derailing Sage's train of thought.

"Who?" Sage half expected his father to say Mick Hillman.

"Do you remember Mom's old friend Lara?" his dad asked. "She and Mom were friends from way back."

"Did she work at the law firm, too?"

"No, nothing like that," his dad said, "but I just thought Mom might have confided stuff in her."

Did his dad seem hurt by the idea that the woman he loved hadn't confided in him and instead told secrets to one of her friends?

"I'm not even sure the names on that list are accurate," Sage said, trying to let his father know there was no shame in not recognizing any of the names on what may very well be a bogus list.

"Well, you could show Lara," his dad suggested. "She and her husband run a yoga studio, not too far from here. She's probably there today." His dad shook his head. "Yoga. I never believed in any of that new-age mumbo jumbo, but your mother was all for it."

Sage wondered if his dad new about the psychic his mom had been seeing. If he thought yoga was new-age mumbo jumbo, he'd love to hear what his dad had to say about psychics, but he decided now was not the time to open up that can of worms.

"Maybe I'll swing by there," Sage said, but then he remembered his car was still parked in front of Rayanne's place. "I don't have my car here, though. Do you think I could borrow yours?"

It reminded him of being younger, back in his college days, when his car seemed to break down every other day. He was constantly borrowing his father's car, a battered old Subaru wagon which was far less cool-looking than his Supra, and far more reliable.

His father was trying to pass his keys to Sage, but Sage was too wrapped up in his thoughts to notice. He was thinking about meeting Melodie at Pleasant Perk when her shift let out. Probably about half the time he met her there, he was driving his dad's less cool Subaru. Was that the vehicle Frances had seen parked in the Pleasant Perk lot that night, or the car she thought she had seen? But what if it had been a different but similar Subaru parked there. Because he knew someone who drove a nearly identical car, someone who had known Melodie and who was especially good at lurking.

"I need to go," Sage said, and he looked up to see his dad's outstretched hand holding the keys.

He didn't bother to explain that he wasn't going to Lara's yoga studio.

43

AS SOON AS Sage got behind the wheel of his father's car, he realized he had a problem. He didn't know where Justin Turner lived. Google proved to be less than helpful. A name like Justin Turner was just a little too common to trust any of the results that came up. But he had something else.

He scrolled through his phone's photos until he found it—the grainy image of the license plate on Justin Turner's Subaru. It was time to return the dozen or so calls Rod had made to him in the last hour.

"Where are you?" Rod asked when he answered the phone. Sage heard the agitation in his voice.

"I'm sorry. I shouldn't have run off on you like that."

"Where are you?" Rod repeated. The anger had brought a tremble to his tone.

"I'm at the hospital," Sage said. Then, realizing his friend might think he was there as a patient, he quickly added, "To visit my mother."

"But how did you get there?" Rod asked.

The question struck Sage as strange, and it took him a moment or two to reply.

"I got an Uber," Sage said. Rod was silent on the other end. "Look, I know you were just trying to help. What I did was shitty—"

"Last night," Rod said, cutting him off, "did Rayanne move your car before she drove you home?"

It was Sage's turn to go silent. He was embarrassed to admit that he didn't entirely recall what happened the previous evening.

"I don't know," he at last admitted. "I don't remember."

On the other end, Rod grunted in reply. Was it his imagination, or was Rod acting kind of strange? What was with his question about Rayanne moving his car? Any other time, Sage might have asked about that, but he didn't really care and didn't have time to get into that.

"Look, I know it's your day off, but I have a huge favor to ask you," Sage said. "I mean, I realize I'm the last person on earth you want to do a favor for right now."

"What is it?" Rod's tone was curt, but Sage took it as a good sign that he hadn't simply hung up. If the roles were reversed, that's probably what Sage would have done.

"I wondered if you could run a plate number. I need an address."

"Go ahead, what's the number?"

"I'll text it to you," Sage said.

"Okay," Rod said. "Give me like ten minutes."

It was ten minutes for Sage to question his motives. He wanted to find his sister's murderer. He wanted it to be Justin Turner, because that would finally bring him the closure he needed. It was easy to believe that the creepy, brick-throwing guy was a murderer. But if so, why had the police missed out on this suspect. Sage reminded himself that the Pleasant Oaks Police Department was staffed by a bunch of incompetent idiots. But at least one of those incompetent idiots had known who Justin Turner was. Could they have really let that murderer slip through their fingers? Or maybe that was precisely why Justin had slipped through their fingers. Sometimes it was all about who you knew, or in the case of Sage's termination, all about who you pissed off.

But there was another reason he was so desperate to prove Justin Turner had murdered his sister. It would exonerate him. He thought of that first post on the web sleuth forum all those years ago that laid out the case for why he was the most likely suspect in his sister's killing. He could still see the username DaddysLilGirl and its cartoon avatar. What bothered him the most about the post was not that it was outlandish, but that it was measured and logical. Of all the theories put forth on who had murdered Melodie Dorian, that one made the most sense. The facts were there. Everything added up.

He knew he hadn't murdered Melodie. Well, he was 99 percent sure he hadn't. Maybe that was more like 95 percent, perhaps an even 90. So maybe things hadn't dropped to 90 until this morning. Until he learned from his friend that he couldn't even accurately remember the events of the previous evening. If his memory couldn't be trusted that far back, could he really be sure of what he had or had not done six years ago? He wouldn't even give it another thought if Melodie's coworker hadn't been so sure he was there that night. He reminded himself that under his questioning she began to second-guess her memory of the evening. That was the whole problem with memory, wasn't it?

But suppose Frances was right, and she had seen him there that night, or thought she had seen him because she saw someone who was about his height, sitting in a car that looked just like one he often drove. Well, that would tie in very nicely with that psycho Justin Turner murdering his sister.

Sage's head was spinning by the time Rod called him back.

"Okay," Rod said. "I got a name and address for you. The name's Virgil Chandler, and the address is . . ."

But Sage didn't hear the address that Rod read off. He had stopped listening at the name Virgil Chandler.

"What did you say the name was?" Sage asked.

"Virgil Chandler," Rod repeated. His words were clear. Sage hadn't imagined it.

A memory from the previous evening came back to him, Rayanne calling out to him as he walked back toward his car, *I hope you have some luck finding Justin!* She had corrected herself after that, said something about Virgil using aliases. A murderer trying to evade the law might use an alias.

He had to get the address again from Rod.

"Listen," Rod said. "There's something I need to—"

"I'll talk to you later," Sage promised. "I have to do this right now."

"Don't do anything stupid," Rod said, and Sage wondered if his friend was thinking about the night he had come and bailed Sage out of the Pleasant Oaks police station.

When he had thought Justin or Virgil or whatever the hell the guy's name was had thrown a brick through his mother's window, he had nearly beat the guy to death with his bare hands. He told himself that this time he wasn't going to lose control like that, but he honestly wasn't sure he could keep that promise to himself. If this man had killed Melodie, would Sage be able to stop himself from attacking him?

When the rage took over, he no longer had any control. It was kind of like being drunk. He had only the foggiest memory of that day he beat up the guy outside his mother's house, and a part of him feared there were other times the rage had taken over that he could no longer remember at all. Had rage caused him to do far worse things than beat up some random guy, and then wiped all recollection of the event from his head?

44

A TEAR ROLLED down Justin's face. He had spent the past several minutes staring at the screen that showed his results from the Human History test. As he hoped, he had relatives out there.

Unfortunately, two of the relative connections had opted to make their information private, which meant Justin knew nothing about them other than the fact that they existed, but one relative, who the system identified as his half sister, had allowed her information to be released publicly. Seeing her name there, Melodie Dorian, was what had brought on the tears.

Even as he sat there physically in his own apartment, mentally he was miles and years away. He recalled the last time he had seen her, that girl with the beautiful smile, his half sister, Melodie. She and an older woman had been walking across the coffee shop parking lot, the two of them talking and laughing about something.

He remembered the feeling of nervousness that paralyzed him. With one hand on the door handle, he tried to will himself to jump out of the car and shout out to her. He didn't want to scare her, but no, that's exactly what he needed to do. She needed to be scared. Danger was lurking out there for her, and she needed to be cautious.

But he had missed his opportunity to deliver the warning that could have saved her. That night she came in for the reading, he had heard what sort of evil lay in store for the happy, pretty girl. Rather than warn her, he had written nonsense down on that piece of paper. He was an idiot, a weak and cowardly idiot.

It wasn't too late, though. There she was. All he had to do was tell her. All he had to do was get out of the car and shout to her. Would she run from him? Would she laugh at him? Those stupid, meaningless questions made him hesitate, and then all hell broke loose.

Justin had never heard a noise like the one that echoed through his head that night. The voices were shouting and screaming all at once, all of them saying different things, each one louder than the next. The noise was unbearable. It felt like his head would explode. He wasn't sure how long it went on. It felt like an eternity. When the screaming had quieted to a dull roar and he could hear himself think again, he looked up and saw that Melodie was gone. His was the only car left in the parking lot. His second opportunity to warn her had passed. It would turn out to be his last, but the truth was, he wasn't thinking about Melodie Dorian anymore.

He was only thinking of his mother, because though it had been difficult to make sense of all the screaming in his head, he heard enough to know he would find his mother at the hospital, and that she needed him desperately.

Now, all these years later, he wondered about that night. In his frantic race to get to the hospital had he passed his half sister's murderer? What if he had swerved his car and caused an accident or run the killer off the road? Could one erratic driving maneuver have saved his half sister's life, and if so, why couldn't the voices have given him some useful advice instead of their cryptic ramblings? What good was his gift if it couldn't save the people he cared about?

When he heard someone pounding on his door, he knew it must be the police. Frankly, he was relieved. He would turn himself in. Confess to anything they wanted him to confess to. They would lock him up, but so what? Wasn't he already in a sort of prison?

Besides, it was what he deserved. He was a coward who failed to protect people even when given advance warning that they were in danger. What right did he have to walk around a free man when his inaction had led to their deaths?

So Justin got up and calmly walked to the door. He undid the lock and pulled the door open. But it wasn't his pal Brick Dick on the other side. It was Sage Dorian. Justin remembered those two other relatives who had shown up on the Human History results, the ones who had opted for privacy. Could Sage Dorian be one of those unknown relatives?

It was Justin's last thought before Sage's fist flew toward him and everything went black.

45

SAGE SWORE BENEATH HIS BREATH. He hadn't meant to punch the guy again, but seeing his face stirred up a roiling sea of emotions, and before he could stop himself, he had taken a swing. It was a good one, and he had caught the other man off guard. Justin went down like a ton of bricks. Sage glanced back over his shoulder, but none of the other complex residents were around.

He stepped in through the open door, careful not to step on the fallen man as he pushed the door closed. He found a towel in the kitchen and some ice cubes in the freezer and fashioned a homemade ice pack. He carried it and a second dampened towel over to where Justin lay. He wiped the fallen man's face with the towel until he stirred back to life, blinking his eyes in confusion. When his eyes finally focused on Sage squatting over him, he panicked and tried to back away, but he was hemmed in by the wall.

"Relax," Sage said. "I'm not going to hurt you. Here." He handed over the ice pack. Still looking confused, the younger man took it and pressed it to his face. "Look, I'm sorry," Sage said. Justin still looked stunned, but Sage was surprised by how calm the other man seemed. If their roles had been reversed, Sage would have tried to attack his intruder. At the very least he would have made more of an effort to get away, but Justin just slumped there on the floor with the ice pack pressed to his face.

"I guess you're probably wondering why some guy you don't even know keeps attacking you," Sage said.

"I know who you are," Justin said. His voice was slightly muffled by the ice pack towel. "You're Melodie's older brother. You think I killed her and hurt your mom."

Sage was impressed. Justin knew more than Sage thought, but Sage realized this put him at a severe disadvantage.

"I'm not even sure I know your name," Sage said.

"Virgil Chandler," the other man said in a stiff, robotic voice.

"So your mother was a prostitute who died when you were a toddler and you grew up in foster care?"

The other man blinked, and though he remained cool and impassive, Sage thought he could detect some confusion and agitation.

"I didn't know that about her being a prostitute," the other man said. He set the ice pack down on the ground but made no move to get up. Sage wondered if he had just delivered some earth-shattering family revelation in a pretty blunt way, but apparently punch first and ask questions later had become his new motto.

Sage rose to his feet and scanned the small apartment. The place looked to be in a state of disarray, but who was he to criticize the cleanliness of someone else's apartment. He noticed the tumbled pile of books, and there, mixed in with the disheveled library, Sage spotted the bricks. Virgil's weapon of choice.

Sage stepped over and dug one of the bricks from the pile. He hefted it in his hand and tried to imagine what it would feel like to fling the brick through a kitchen window or at a young woman standing in the driveway.

"Real tough guy," Sage muttered.

"Sorry?" Virgil said.

"Go around throwing bricks at people from the safety of your car."

"I didn't throw any bricks," Virgil said. "I think someone tried to frame me."

"You know what I think?" Sage said. "I don't think your real name is Virgil Chandler." Sage stood back over the slumped man, smacking the brick into his open palm. "I think you murdered the real Virgil Chandler, then set his car on fire. I think you murdered him, like you murdered Melodie and my mother."

"No," the other man said. He shook his head vigorously back and forth. He was crying. Sage felt no pity for Virgil or Justin or whatever his name was. He felt only disgust.

"What about Ambrose Radcliffe?" Sage asked. "Did you kill him too?"

"Who?" Virgil said.

Sage wondered what had happened to his old friend Ambrose Radcliffe. Of course, he didn't really think of him as Ambrose. He thought of him as PhillyFury. That was the thing about the online world, everyone hid behind different names on the internet. Fake names, fake avatars. The web sleuth forums were as full of phonies as anywhere else online. Rayanne was probably right that there were plenty of perps hanging out there, curious to see if anyone could piece together the truth about their devious deeds. Was that how this cowardly loser had found Ambrose?

"Maybe you know him as PhillyFury," Sage said.

"Virgil?" the man asked.

"No!" Sage screamed, frustrated. He forced himself to set the brick down on a small folding table before he lost his cool and smacked this guy in the head with it. The guy had pretty much admitted to not being Virgil Chandler, but before Sage had a chance to fully grasp this, something else caught his attention, a piece of paper on the folding table that bore a familiar logo. It looked like Virgil Chandler had gotten some results from the good folks at Human History. Only, he reminded himself, these results were not for Virgil Chandler, because as Sage was now 99 percent sure, Virgil Chandler had been murdered six years ago before being burned in a stolen car.

"She was my sister," Justin said. He had finally risen to his feet and now stood a couple of feet from Sage, looking over Sage's shoulder at the results letter from Human History. "My own sister, and I didn't save her. I failed to protect her."

The words were familiar to Sage because some version of them had been playing over and over in his own head for the past six years.

"Your half sister," Sage said when he at last made sense of the information in front of him.

"The only family I have," Justin said. Then he corrected himself, "The only family I had."

Sage studied the genetic match results. Melodie's was the only name listed. The other two users had opted to keep their results private. He was one, but who was the other? It struck him that whoever they were, their decision to keep their results private might save their life. Whoever had murdered his sister and Virgil Chandler wouldn't be able to track down this anonymous person to kill them too.

"Not the only family," Sage reminded him. He pointed at one of the anonymized matches on the results list. Then he turned to the other man, his half brother, and recalled what had brought him racing out here. "You were there that night."

He didn't have to say where or when. Justin knew what he was talking about. He nodded.

"I . . ." Justin hesitated. "I had a premonition that something bad was going to happen to her. I should have warned her."

Sage didn't have much use for premonitions, but it called up a memory of a police sketch artist drawing based on a young psychic's description of a murderer. Ultimately, it had led to Sage solving Culver Creek's infamous cold case. He remembered his conversation with Eloise, the funeral parlor director, and her surprise that a psychic woman had been hit by a bus. He heard something else Eloise had said. *He was a good kid. I mean, a little strange.* Eloise had blamed Justin's strangeness on growing up in a fortune teller's parlor, but what if that wasn't it.

"You were the psychic one," Sage said. "Not your mother."

"We worked together," Justin said defensively, then he seemed to realized his error. "You know about my mother?"

"She was killed the same night my sister was," Sage said.

"I tried to warn her," Justin said, "but in the end, I couldn't save either of them."

Sage understood the frustration. It was something else the two of them had in common. It wasn't the only thing. Sage looked at the brick he had set down on the table. Justin thought someone was trying to frame him. Sage thought of Colin Hillman showing up outside Sage's apartment with the name Jillian Werks. If you can't murder your half siblings, then frame them for murder.

"It was all Virgil Chandler's fault," Justin said. "He got picked up by the police, but he had a fake driver's license with my name on it. They called my mother, and she went racing down there because she thought I was in trouble."

"But you weren't at the police station," Sage said. "You were following my sister."

Justin shook his head.

"Just sitting in my car in the parking lot. I should have warned her, but I was too afraid, and then my mother . . ." Justin's voice trailed off, and he walked away from the table, into the little galley kitchen.

Melodie had been murdered after her Human History results came in. That meant the murderer must be the other anonymous half sibling. Colin Hillman was the obvious answer, but couldn't it be anyone? Every time he turned around he seemed to stumble over another half sibling. For a while there he had even assumed Zoey was one of them.

Zoey. The thought hit him like the pile of bricks that lay tumbled on the ground with Justin's books. He picked up the envelope that Justin's Human History results had been sent in, but he already knew what he would see. The postmark was from only a few days ago. Justin, or Virgil Chandler as his Human History account identified him, hadn't been in the system back when someone hurled a brick at Zoey Wilson in his mother's driveway. Someone *was* trying to frame Virgil/Justin, but it wasn't because he had completed the Human History test.

Justin stepped out of the kitchen, and there was a strange look on his face. Just seeing it made Sage queasy. Maybe he had just a little bit of those psychic powers that Justin had, because he already knew what Justin was going to say.

"Do you have a wife?" Justin asked. "Or maybe a girlfriend?"

"She's in danger, isn't she?" Sage asked.

Justin nodded.

"Come on, let's go," Sage said.

46

WHEN SAGE PULLED up outside Zoey's apartment, Justin shook his head.

"She's not here," Justin said.

"Her father will be," Sage said. "He'll know where to find her."

On the drive, he had tried to call her multiple times, first from his phone, then Justin's. All the calls went to voicemail, which Sage didn't like one bit. It wasn't like her to dodge calls from potential clients.

It seemed to be taking Victor Wilson an eternity to answer the door. Sage shifted his weight nervously from foot to foot. Justin stood beside him, seemingly untroubled. When he finally opened the door, Zoey's father looked the exact opposite of untroubled.

"What are you doing here?" Victor growled. "Hasn't she been through enough?"

The man started to close the door, and it was Justin whose quick reflexes caught it before it slammed shut.

"She's in danger," Justin said. "We need to know where she is."

"Who are you?" Victor asked. "His new partner?"

Sage didn't have time for this.

"Zoey's in trouble," Sage said. "We need to know where she is!"

"She can take care of herself," Victor said.

"Sure, fine, whatever," Sage said. "Maybe try calling her then, to make sure she's okay."

"She probably has her phone off," Victor said.

Sage felt uneasy, well, more uneasy. It felt like Victor was stalling him, and he didn't like it. The man had been locked up for years for murder but was recently released when his conviction was overturned on faulty DNA evidence. It had come to light that Zoey's sister was the actual murderer, but there was always the chance a mistake had been made again, and maybe Victor was not the innocent man he pretended to be.

"She turned off her phone to be polite?" Justin asked.

Victor nodded. He looked uncertainly from Justin to Sage. Sage didn't understand what was going on.

"This is a big opportunity for her," Victor said. "I don't want the likes of you messing it up for her."

"The man from TV will be there," Justin said.

Victor nodded again, a little more slowly. It was like he and Justin were having some private conversation.

"Someone want to tell me what the hell is going on?" Sage asked.

"She's at the golf course?" Justin said, but it came out like a question.

For a moment, Sage didn't understand how Justin had gotten this information out of the frustrating conversation with Victor Wilson, but then Sage understood. Justin was relying on his psychic gifts to get this information. Victor was just confirming what Justin had already guessed at.

Justin grabbed hold of Sage's arm and started to tug him back toward the car.

"We need to go," Justin said. "We need to go now!"

As Sage raced toward the country club, doubts began to take over his mind. If Zoey was in trouble and at the country club, then didn't that suggest Colin or maybe Mick Hillman was the threat? So he called Rod.

When voicemail picked up, Sage hesitated. Rod already thought he was nuts and an alcoholic, and he feared that any message he left would only confirm all of Rod's suspicions. So Sage did his best to keep his tone level and calm, but he couldn't help the words from rushing out as he tried to explain everything to his friend.

"Listen," Sage said when he hung up the phone. "They're probably not going to let us in there."

"You can go in the back way," Justin suggested.

Sage pulled his attention away from the road for a moment to study his companion. How did Justin know about the back entrance?

"There's a driveway for the employees," Justin said. "And a door that goes into the kitchen from back by the dumpster."

"You worked here?" Sage asked.

"I had to stop after Virgil was killed," Justin said.

The chain was off the employee driveway when Sage pulled up it. He drove too fast up the rough road and turned the sharp corner that led to the banquet hall, but he was forced to slam on the brakes. A familiar silver car sat blocking their way.

47

SAGE PULLED the car up in the area behind the country club after maneuvering around the empty silver sedan. As soon as he shut off the ignition, he jumped out of the car and Justin started to follow him, but Sage held up a hand to stop him.

"Wait," Sage said. "I need you to go in through the front door."

"They won't let me in." Justin looked down at his T-shirt and jeans. Even if there wasn't a private function going on, he didn't meet the country club's dress code standards.

"Exactly," Sage said.

"But I want you to give them a hard time," Sage said. "Put up a fight."

Justin recalled hunkering there in front of Melodie's house as Sage's fists pounded away at him. Putting up a fight wasn't exactly his specialty, and Sage must have realized this because he made a resigned sighing noise.

"Just stall them for as long as you can. Wait for them to bring out the reinforcements," Sage said. "I want as many of the staff and security guards at the front of the building as possible."

Justin nodded. It was a good plan. Maybe it might actually work.

~

J ustin's hands shook as he opened the building's front door. He expected right away that someone would start yelling at him to leave. Once, back when he had worked as a dishwasher, he saw a man whose membership had lapsed get roughly marched out of the building by one of the guards. They took security pretty seriously at the Pleasant Oaks Country Club, and Justin could only assume that at a private event for a well-known politician the security would be extra tight.

That was why he was shocked when he was able to walk right in the front door. No one seemed to be on duty. He looked around the little entryway, but it was deserted. Sage had said he wanted as many staff and security guards at the front of the building as possible. This was a very bad sign.

Justin took a few steps around. As a dishwasher he had spent precious little time at the front of the building and was expressly forbidden from interacting with members. That was why he was stunned when he noticed a photo of a familiar face hanging on the wall. Justin couldn't help but stare. There were two familiar faces in the old photo, Melodie and her boyfriend. Justin couldn't help recalling the night the two of them had wandered into his mom's shop all giggles and smiles. Seeing their smiling faces hung up on the wall, he felt like someone was stabbing him in the chest.

The sound of approaching voices startled him, and he panicked and looked around for a place to hide. He had forgotten all about Sage's request that he cause a scene and stall the staff. He just wanted to lay low, and the deserted coat check closet looked like the perfect hiding place. Justin dashed inside, burrowing into a rack of jackets as he held his breath and listened to the approaching voices.

"Where's Lisa?" a woman asked. "She was supposed to be out here."

"Something's not right," a man said.

NOTHING'S RIGHT! Justin nearly gasped when the screaming voice filled his head. Of course the voices would pick this moment to start chattering, but this was way more than their normal chatter. He was reminded of the night his mother was killed. It was almost that loud. *They'll see you. You're not invisible.*

Justin realized the voices were right. The coat check closet was only so big, and he was hardly hidden. But he had an idea. He grabbed one of the jackets off a hanger—a wool sport coat— and threw it on. The sleeves were comically short, but it wasn't like he had time to be choosy. In fact, he had gotten his borrowed jacket on just in time.

"Hey!" Standing at the coat check window were a man and woman dressed in the country club's polo shirt and khakis uniform. The pair he had been trying to listen to before the voices started shouting at him. "You're new here, aren't you?"

Justin nodded mutely at the woman asking him questions.

"I need you to cover Lisa's stand until she gets back." The woman pointed at the empty hostess stand planted in front of the entryway door.

"And don't let anyone in who isn't on the list," the man barked at him.

Justin nodded again. He could hardly believe this. His stupid disguise was working. He didn't even have one of the uniform shirts on, but he guessed they assumed he was a new employee who hadn't yet been issued a polo shirt.

"You didn't see where Lisa went, did you?" the woman asked as Justin stepped behind the hostess stand.

Sweat poured out of him, and he knew it wasn't just because of the wool sport coat. He figured he was seconds away from getting busted. He was about to point back toward the closed dining room doors, but he remembered what Sage had said.

"Outside," Justin said in a quavering voice. He pointed at the front door.

"Goddamnit," the man muttered, and Justin was relieved to see the pair of them step out the front doors.

But there was no time to catch his breath. The voices commenced their screaming.

It's too late to save him! You should have warned him! There was no one around, but Justin glanced at the closed dining room doors all the same. Had something happened to Sage Dorian? But he had been listening to the confusing messages from the voices long enough to know he shouldn't assume that was who they were talking about.

The ghost girl is in trouble! Help the ghost girl!

Justin looked instinctively at the wall where Melodie's photo hung. Was she the ghost girl the voices were talking about? But how could he save Melodie? He had his chance to save her, and he'd failed. But if Melodie wasn't the ghost girl the voices were chattering about, then who?

"Where is she?" Justin asked, even though he knew the voices wouldn't answer him. But it turned out he didn't need the voices.

A woman's scream rang out from a distant corner of the building. It sounded like it had come from the long hallway that ran past the main dining room. Justin ran toward it.

A lthough it was a relief that there was no more screaming, he would have appreciated some sort of noise to guide him in the right direction. There were doors that led off the hallway. The screaming could have come from behind any of them or none of them. Justin wished he had a clue.

It's the cop! Justin turned around at the shouting in his head, half expecting to see Brick Dick standing there. But the hallway was deserted, and as he grabbed one of the doors and flung it open, it occurred to Justin that Sage had been a cop as well, but he forgot all about this when he looked down to see what was stopping the door from opening all the way and saw a man lying there on the ground. Ambrose Radcliffe, his case-worker, and judging by the grayish tinge to his skin and the bloody bullet hole in the man's forehead, it was safe to say that Ambrose Radcliffe was very much not alive.

48

SAGE STEPPED into the crowded dining room wearing an ill-fitting waiter's uniform. The spare uniforms had been exactly where Justin said they would be. If only his sister's murderer would be as easy to locate, but as Sage scanned the packed room, he could tell he was going to have a problem.

There were an astounding amount of people milling about the room. It was hard to believe that the unlikeable senator could have so many supporters, but then you didn't get elected without being popular. Sage wondered how many of these people would withdraw their support once they knew about the senator's ugly personal life, but he feared there would be a shocking number who would still stand by the man even after learning the truth. It turned his stomach.

Sage scanned the sea of faces looking for a familiar one. Waiters moved among the crowded room with trays of appetizers and trays of wine. He realized his mistake just as an angry-looking woman bore down on him.

"You're not getting paid to stand around and look pretty," she said to him.

"I'm sorry," Sage muttered as he turned to go back into the kitchen for a tray, but a hand on his arm stopped him.

The woman had grabbed hold of his sleeve, and he turned back to face her. She scrutinized him with narrowed eyes.

"Who the hell are you?" she demanded. "You're not the new guy!"

Sage pulled his arm free from her grasp and ran into the sea of people. His best bet was to lose himself in the crowd, but on more than one occasion he had seen the country club security staff in action, and he knew he was in trouble.

Maybe it was a mistake to try to handle this all on his own, but he didn't see what other choice he had. No one was going to listen to him, and there was no time to waste. He just hoped he wasn't too late.

He glanced over his shoulder and saw the waitstaff supervisor talking to a tall angry-looking man. Sage recognized the guy as one of Mick Hillman's own security guards. Crap.

Sage threaded his way quickly through the crowd. He glanced back and saw the security guard headed his way, a cell phone in his hand. Reinforcements would be on their way soon. Sage did another quick visual sweep of the room, but he didn't see his sister's murderer in the crowd. So he followed his instincts and ran to the exit doors before they got sealed off.

S age heard the dining room doors open behind him, and he ducked into a short, dark hallway. He pressed himself into a closed doorway and held his breath as two security guards ran down the longer hall.

He heard two men speaking, but it wasn't the guards. It sounded like it was coming from the other side of the door he leaned against. Clearly he had picked a crappy hiding place. It took him a moment to realize he recognized both of the men's voices. One from the endless television campaign commercials that endeavored to make him sound like the second coming of Christ, and the other most recently from an underhanded attempt to get Sage arrested. Both Mick's and Colin's voices made him sick to his stomach, but he didn't dare move with the guards so close. At any point, one or both of them would double back and check out this little hallway.

"What are you, some kind of idiot?" Mick shouted. "No one's calling the cops."

"But we have to do something," Colin said.

Sage had a pretty good idea of who the security guard had called on his cell phone. It didn't surprise him that Colin was in favor of calling the police to deal with the intruder, but it surprised him that the big man himself didn't seem interested in locking Sage up.

"You know what happens if the papers get ahold of this?" Mick asked. Ah, now Sage understood. Mick didn't want to call the police because he was too worried about his reputation and how it would look to have someone like Sage arrested at his swanky victory celebration.

Sage heard laughter. Was it Colin's? Had Mick told some joke or made some wisecrack in a voice too quiet for Sage to hear. The laughter stopped abruptly.

"The papers," Colin said. "Your precious image. You disgust me."

"And tell me, do those checks I write you every week also disgust you?"

"Now that you mention it, yes. Yes, they do."

"Well, here's your chance to actually earn your paycheck. Make him disappear," Mick said in a menacing tone.

"This is a human being we're talking about," Colin said.

"That's not my problem," Mick snarled.

Half a second later, Sage heard a door slam closed. Sage hoped that meant the room Mick and Colin were in had another door and that both men had taken it. He pressed his ear to the door to try to hear any movement on the other side. Then he heard movement, not from the other side of the door but from the hallway. Footsteps approached. He glanced around, but there was nowhere else to hide. He pushed open the door and hoped he wasn't stepping right into the lion's den. He pulled it closed behind him and locked it from the inside.

Sage found himself in some sort of stockroom, and Colin and Mick Hillman were nowhere in sight. He let out the breath he had been holding, took a step over toward one of the shelves in the room, but tripped over something on the floor. He grabbed hold of the shelf to steady himself, silently praying he hadn't made enough noise to be heard by the security guards hunting for him. He looked down at the ground to see what he had tripped over, and froze in alarm.

Ambrose Radcliffe, aka PhillyFury, stared up at him with dead, unseeing eyes. And now the conversation he overhead between Mick and Colin made more sense. The two men hadn't been discussing him. They were discussing Ambrose.

Sage tried to work out what had happened. Ambrose must have figured out the Unknown Suitor case, or almost figured it out. Had Ambrose come here to ask Mick Hillman if the Unknown Suitor, Virgil Chandler, was Mick's illegitimate child? Had Mick shot the man in the head himself or did he have one of his security goons do it for him? No, probably not one of the goons. Not with a matter as delicate as this. The thing with powerful people was that they always thought they could get away with anything, but Sage figured their reasoning was pretty sound. They did get away with so much stuff.

"What the hell are you doing here?"

Sage looked up and saw that Colin had returned to the

little storeroom. He was carrying a tarp and rope in his hand. Before Sage could speak, the door handle behind him jiggled. The security guards. Did they have a key? If not, how long before they could procure one? Sage figured that at most he had about ten seconds. Colin watched the jiggling handle with alarm.

"Quick," Colin said. "Come with me." He motioned for Sage to follow him back in the direction he'd just come from.

"Why? So you can do to me what you did to poor Ambrose here?" Sage asked.

"Fine," Colin said. "Then deal with them yourself."

So with mixed feelings, Sage picked what he hoped was the lesser of two evils and followed Colin out of the stockroom. The lights were off, but some light streamed in from the windows, and Sage could see mannequins in golf shirts and a display of golf clubs. They were in the country club's pro shop.

Colin motioned him toward the other end of the store. Sage followed him. He watched the storeroom door, but the handle didn't move. Probably the guards had been distracted by Ambrose's dead body.

"I didn't have anything to do with that dead man," Colin said.

"Sorry if I have trouble believing you after that hot tip you gave me," Sage said.

"Look, if it's any consolation, I was duped too," Colin said.

"Sure, sure, and you're a saint who's never done anything wrong. You met my sister, while innocently getting a coffee, and you've never told a lie in your life. They should make you a saint. Saint Colin. Or would that be Saint Virgil?"

"You were spying on me?" Colin asked.

"You're a suspicious dude," Sage said. "I guess apples don't fall far from trees."

"Don't say that," Colin said. "I'm nothing like him."

"You can drop the Boy Scout routine," Sage said. "I know all about Pleasant Perk's side business."

"It's not what you think," Colin said.

"I have it on good authority that Virgil Chandler is a regular."

"Shh!" Colin hissed at him.

Sage opened his mouth to call Colin out on being a liar and a scumbag, but then he saw the stockroom doorknob turn. Colin motioned for Sage to get behind the table of folded shirts.

As Sage peered over the top of a chartreuse golf shirt, he saw Colin step toward the door just as one of the security goons stepped into the shop. The security guard aimed a gun at Colin.

"It's me," Colin said, and the gun went back into its holster. "I just searched this whole place. He's not in here. I think he might be hiding in the kitchen."

From his hiding spot, Sage watched as Colin followed the security guard back into the stockroom, closing the door behind him. Sage let out the breath he had been holding.

He stood up, turned around and found himself looking into Zoey's eyes.

49

JUSTIN STOOD at the sink in the swanky men's room patting his face dry with a paper towel. He had washed all the vomit flecks off his face, but the taste was still in his mouth. The man beside him was dressed in a suit that looked like it cost a lot of money, and Justin felt the man's eyes on him.

He glanced over at the man, and the guy smiled politely at Justin.

"Are you a nephew?" the man asked.

"Nephew?" Justin repeated.

"Sorry, I just thought I saw some family resemblance," the man said. "I think I probably had one too many cocktails."

He's going to die, the voices said. *He's going to die. They're all going to die.*

"Everyone dies," Justin said quietly, but the man was still standing there.

"Sorry?" he asked.

"Everyone does," Justin corrected. "Have too many cocktails, I mean."

The man nodded and chuckled politely, but Justin saw the

way he quickly moved toward the door, keeping one eye on the crazy man. He wasn't offended. Stuff like that happened to him all the time.

"Hey!" Justin called out as the man opened the door. He froze there in the doorway in his expensive suit. "Uh, be careful out there tonight."

The man gave him the slow nod that said *I'm dealing with a crazy man.* He didn't blame the guy. It wasn't even a useful warning. If he knew how the man was supposed to die, he could be more specific and tell him not to drive himself home or to avoid those buffalo wings they were serving so he didn't choke on a bone. But the he's-going-to-die message didn't tell him much of anything.

"Thanks for nothing," Justin said when the man had left and he was alone in the bathroom.

Justin stuck his head beneath the tap and filled his mouth with water, swishing it around to try to clean out the vomit taste.

THEY'RE ALL GOING TO DIE!

The extra loud shouting from the voices was followed by a sound so loud it made Justin spit out his mouthful of water, spraying it all over the mirror and counter.

"What the hell, man?" With all the commotion in his head, he hadn't heard someone else enter the men's room. But it didn't matter, he was in no shape to pretend like everything was fine. He ran past the man and out into the hall, his heart pounding.

The voices were screaming in his head. It sounded like gibberish.

She wears a string of pearls around her harbor. They're all going to die! She sure looks pretty in Oklahoma City. They're all going to die! We must go to Manhattan to finish the project. They're all going to die!

Places seemed to be the connection between all the different gibberish: Pearl Harbor, Oklahoma City, Manhattan. No, not random places. Places where tragedies had happened— the attack on Pearl Harbor, the Oklahoma City bombing, September 11th. And of course that fit with the whole they're-all-going-to-die theme, but it still didn't give him much in the way of specifics. There was more gibberish, but he was trying to play back what the voices had said, even as they shouted more place names.

We must go to Manhattan to finish the project. The Manhattan Project, that's what they had called the building of the atomic bomb. And Pearl Harbor and Oklahoma City had both been bombed. As he listened to the other place names being shouted by the voices, he recognized them as other places that had been bombed or had something to do with bombs.

50

"ZOEY!" Sage cried out. "You're okay." But even as he said the words, he saw her shaking her head violently. A second later, he felt cool metal against his neck.

"Step away from her real slow," a familiar voice said in his ear.

He could have protested that he hadn't meant Zoey any harm, but he knew there was no point because he recognized the voice that had spoken in his ear. The one from the person who now held the barrel of a handgun against his neck. It belonged to Rayanne Lawrence.

Sage held his hands up and stepped slowly backward. He didn't want to do anything to startle Rayanne. As he stepped away, he noticed something he had missed before. Zoey's hands were bound behind her back, and a ring of duct tape bound her ankles together.

"You need to let her go," Sage said. "She doesn't have anything to do with this."

"Quite the contrary," Rayanne said. "She has everything to do with it."

But Sage knew Rayanne was mistaken. It was an error only someone consulting the official police DNA database would have made, and it all stemmed from the fact that when Zoey and her sister were kids and their DNA samples were taken as part of the investigation into the murder of their babysitter, the samples were reversed.

"She's not Hillman's daughter," Sage said. "It's her sister you want."

"You're not a very good liar," Rayanne said.

She stood between him and Zoey, the gun still trained on him.

"It's the truth," Sage said. "Their samples got switched."

A look of doubt crossed her face. Would this doubt and confusion be enough to get her to let her guard down? He prayed it would be, but like him, Rayanne was a trained professional. Size and strength were on his side, and if Zoey hadn't been there, he probably would have taken his chances and charged at Rayanne, but he wasn't comfortable putting Zoey's life at risk that way. It was a miracle Rayanne hadn't killed Zoey, but Sage had a theory about that, and it all went back to a post on the web sleuth forum years ago. In terms of framing him, Rayanne had been playing the long game.

"You broke into my apartment and planted those alcohol bottles," Sage said.

"You made my job that much easier when you decided to stick them in your car," Rayanne said.

Sage remembered why he had placed the alcohol bottles there, and he shook his head in disgust.

"You killed Giselle," Sage said.

"She knew too much, and she was starting to ask questions," Rayanne said.

"And what about Melodie?" Sage asked. "Did she know too much too? Is that why you murdered her?"

His eyes flicked over to Zoey. He wished there was some way he could indicate to her that she should try to work herself free from her bonds.

"You know where I grew up?" Rayanne asked.

"Culver Creek?" Sage asked. He watched Rayanne's hand. Her grip on the handgun had loosened an almost imperceptible amount.

"That's right, the butt crack of Pennsylvania," Rayanne said. "But yeah, not only that. I grew up in an old, run-down, mold-infested trailer. Meanwhile Melodie, she's living the good life, isn't she? Grows up in swanky Pleasant Oaks, spends her time hob-knobbing with the well-to-do at the Pleasant Oaks Country Club. She's dating Mick Hillman's son, which is all pretty sick when you think about it."

"She didn't know they were related," Sage said, unable to stop himself from defending his sister.

"Yeah, right," Rayanne said. "I know an opportunistic bitch when I see one."

"You don't know the first thing about my sister," Sage said.

He was relieved that Rayanne was so focused on him. It meant she didn't see Zoey squirming around as she tried to free her bound wrists.

"She didn't even know about Hillman," Sage said. "That information was kept secret from us."

"Secret from you, maybe," Rayanne said, "but you can be damn sure your spoiled sister knew. Virgil Chandler told her."

"She didn't even know—"

"That little weasel went looking for information on his dead mother. Struck paydirt when he found out she had been prostituting herself to Mick Hillman, and then did some more digging because the more dirt you have, the more money you can get when you blackmail someone."

So Virgil Chandler had apparently worked out details

about the family tree long before Sage had. It was no accident, then, that he had stolen Justin Turner's identity. Had he also gone into the coffee shop and told Melodie the truth about who her father was? She wouldn't have been sure it was true, of course, so that was why she had gone and paid good money for those Human History tests.

"And you found all this out when you were trailing him," Sage said. "But why murder Melodie?"

"Let me explain something about blackmail to you," Rayanne said. "You can't hold a secret over someone's head if it isn't a secret anymore."

"You were getting a cut of Virgil's blackmail payments," Sage said. "Well, until you killed him and took over the whole thing."

"It was just easier that way," Rayanne said. "Your little sister was planning on making the whole thing public. She was going to go to the press and expose the 'family values' senator for the piece of shit he really was, she was just waiting 'til her boyfriend, aka her half brother, was out of the country so he didn't have to deal with all the fallout. Such a nice, considerate girl."

Tears were welling up in his eyes, because it was true. Melodie was a nice, considerate girl, the nicest, and this monster standing in front of him had murdered her.

"Despising that shithead Hillman is one thing Melodie and I had in common, but I couldn't risk losing my meal ticket."

"You pulled her over in your cruiser that night," Sage said.

"Nice girls pull over when the cops flash their lights," she said. "Even late at night. Isn't that right, Zoey?"

Rayanne turned toward Zoey, and Sage saw his opportunity. He grabbed Rayanne's wrist, but instead of dropping the gun like he had hoped, she tightened her grip on it. She tried to turn it toward him, not easy to do with the grip he had on her wrist. He yanked hard on her arm, but she had no intention of dropping the gun. Then her other fist swung forward and pounded him in the side of the head. It caught him off guard, and he blinked in surprise. It also made him loosen his grip on her wrist ever so slightly, and it was the opportunity she had been waiting for.

She pulled free and spun on him, the gun gripped firmly in both hands and only two inches from his face. He steeled himself for the inevitable. Fate had other plans.

Zoey, who had freed her bound hands, grabbed the first weapon she could find, a golf club with a lethal-looking metal head, and raised it up in the air. She brought it down hard on Rayanne's head. Rayanne slumped to the ground, and at last the gun fell to the floor.

"Oh my god!" Zoey said. "Did I kill her?"

Sage could see the monster still lived.

"Alas, no," he said. "Do you know where that tape is she used on you?"

As Sage watched her, Rayanne began to stir. The gun! He kicked it as far away as he could, and it spun across the floor. Zoey, whose ankles were still bound, had managed to shimmy herself over to retrieve the roll of duct tape and now thrust it at him.

As Sage wrapped the tape around her wrists, Rayanne's eyes blinked open.

"Go ahead, tie me up," Rayanne said. "It will only make it that much easier to prove that you're the murderer."

"That's not going to happen," Sage said.

"I came here when I realized you had kidnapped your mother's real estate agent and that amateur detective who figured out you were the one who murdered your sister. You've been doing a lot of kidnapping lately, like that poor high school girl you abducted the other day."

"You gave that anonymous tip to the Hillman campaign," Sage said. "And you made sure I didn't get locked up because you needed me to be free."

"You're a pretty good detective," Rayanne said. "I'll give you that. Maybe not one of the most astute members of the web sleuth forum, but a little hyperbole now and then never hurt anyone."

Sage remembered the phrasing. It had been in the private message he received from another forum member who had alerted him, months ago, to the job posting for a detective in Culver Creek. The username hadn't been DaddysLilGirl. He would have remembered that, which was probably why Rayanne used multiple accounts on the forum.

"You sent that job listing," Sage said.

"Oh, I did more than that," Rayanne said. "I fought tooth and nail to get them to create a detective position in Culver Creek." She really did play the long game.

"What about Ambrose?" Sage asked.

"Good old PhillyFury." Rayanne laughed and gave a shake of her head. "Goddamn DNA. His crack team of web sleuths was getting too close to the truth for comfort."

"So you killed them," Sage said. "You killed all of them."

"No, that was you. At least, that's what I'll explain to the authorities. It was all part of your dastardly plan to bomb the senator and all the attendees at his big victory party because you're a drunken psycho who wanted to take out your vengeance on the man who got you fired and who fathered you out of wedlock."

"It's a nice story," Sage said with a grunt as he wrapped more tape than was necessary around Rayanne's ankles, just because he could.

"And it's not the first time you tried to crash one of his country club parties, is it? You really made this all too easy,

Sage. Ordering those explosive materials from your computer when I broke into your apartment was just the finishing touch."

Explosive materials? Did that mean her bomb comment hadn't just been the rantings of a madwoman?

"What bomb?" Sage asked.

"It's all part of the reckless behavior you've been displaying for months, beating up some random guy because you thought he had thrown a brick through your mother's window—"

"It was you!" Zoey yelled. "You were the one who threw a brick at me."

"Oh, hardly," Rayanne said. "It was Justin Turner, the real Justin Turner. Because when he found out from his caseworker, a Mr. Ambrose Radcliffe, that Sage was the one who had murdered the girl he was obsessed with, he lost his shit. It will all be there in the notes on Ambrose's computer when the police do their investigation."

"But Justin will be able to tell them the truth," Sage said.

"Right, because the testimony of certified lunatics is always taken extremely seriously." Rayanne laughed like the certified lunatic she was.

"What bomb?" Sage said, repeating his earlier question.

"Oh, that," Rayanne said. "Pish posh. It's far too late to do anything about it now. I do believe it should be going off in another minute or so."

She could be lying, but Sage couldn't take that chance. He grabbed Zoey's shoulder.

"I need you to get out of the building, run out to the parking lot," he instructed.

"What about you?" she asked.

"I'm going to try and clear everyone out of the dining room."

"I'm not leaving without you," Zoey said.

"Oh, what a pair of tragic lovebirds you two are," Rayanne

said. Her laughter sounded like the cackle of an evil witch. Sage ignored her.

"Go out to the parking lot now," Sage said to Zoey, his voice stern. "If I don't make it out, I need someone to tell the truth about what happened here, and to make sure she doesn't get away with this." He gave a disgusted nod in Rayanne's direction.

Her bound ankles were taped to a shelving unit. She wasn't going anywhere soon.

There was a tear in Zoey's eye as she bit her lip and nodded at him. He ran back to the hall, glancing over his shoulder only once to make sure Zoey was headed toward the exit door.

S age burst through the doors of the dining room and stopped short. For a moment he thought he must be in the wrong room, but Mick Hillman campaign posters decorated the room. It was the right room, but it was completely empty. Some scattered cocktail napkins on the carpeted floor were the only sign that a crowd had been here minutes ago.

"Sage Dorian."

Sage had to revise his previous assessment. The room wasn't completely empty. Mick Hillman stood up from the chair where he had been sitting.

"Where is everyone?" Sage asked.

"Oh, didn't you hear?" Mick asked. "Some nutter who used to work here called in a bomb threat."

Justin, Sage thought.

"What are you still doing here?" Sage asked.

"I'm not afraid of imaginary bombs," the senator said. "Or maybe it's a real one, that would be nice, wouldn't it? Go out in a blaze of glory. It beats the alternative."

"Living?"

"Public scorn, ridicule. It's all over."

"We should really get out of here, sir."

Mick Hillman acted like he hadn't heard him. "My son, my own son, has spent the past several months gathering his evidence, all so he could go to the press and make all my dirty laundry public."

That had been Melodie's plan, and Sage was heartened to hear that Colin was going to make it happen. He had underestimated his half brother. He was a stand-up guy after all, and what's more, he was a pretty good actor. He knew the truth about his father, and likely Sage and Melodie, long before Sage had ever sat down in his office. No doubt Rayanne had found out what Colin was up to, maybe she had even tried to kill him with her shotgun through the window trick, but Colin was better protected than the others, so she had to go with Plan B— pin everything on Sage Dorian, and then blow everything up.

"We need to leave," Sage said.

"Go run away with the others," Hillman said. "I'm not afraid of imaginary bombs."

But Justin had been the one who made the call about the bomb. Sage didn't want to believe in psychics any more than the senator wanted to believe in imaginary bombs, but Sage had solved Culver Creek's notorious cold case in part because a psychic little girl had given a police sketch artist a spot-on description of the man who murdered Lily Esposito. Justin had known that Melodie was going to be killed but hadn't been able to save her. So if he called in to report a bomb, Sage had to believe there really was one here.

"I'm not leaving without you," Sage said.

Sage grabbed hold of the senator's arm, and if the senator hadn't been so demoralized at the thought of his entire career going down the toilet, he might have put up more of a fight. He was a battered and broken man, though. So Sage had little problem leading him out of the room and out the front door, even though Mick Hillman was as big as he was.

A second later, a tremendous force knocked both men off their feet.

51

SAGE SAT on the curb in the country club parking lot, holding a wad of paper towels to the gash on his forehead. He got that beauty when the bomb's shockwave knocked him off his feet and he skidded across the asphalt on his forehead. The EMTs wanted to take him to the hospital for treatment, but he had waved them off.

He watched as the ambulance they had loaded Mick Hillman into drove off. The senator looked like he might have broken a bone or two during his scuffle with the parking lot's asphalt, but he would be okay physically. The same could not be said for his career, which when Colin's meticulously gathered evidence hit the press tomorrow most certainly headed for complete and total annihilation.

"You could have been killed!" Zoey shouted at him. She had just returned from getting looked over by the EMTs with a few fresh bandages on her arms.

"I made it out mostly unscathed," he said.

She rolled her eyes at him. "You know I'm beginning to

think that hanging out with you might be hazardous to my health," she said.

"You have a point," he said. "If you didn't want to have anything to do with me, I would understand."

"Oh, you're not getting rid of me that easily." She smiled at him.

He looked up at her standing over him, and even with her face smudged with dirt and her hair a tangled mess, he thought she was one of the most beautiful women on the planet.

"If Rayanne has her way, they'll bring me in on murder and terrorism charges," he said.

"I'm going to go give a statement." She nodded over at where the police cars were congregated. "You coming?"

"In a minute," he said, and as he watched her walk away, he felt giddy with happiness. He hadn't felt like that in a long time.

He glanced back toward the building. The fire department had already extinguished the flames, and now the partially collapsed building sat there smoldering. The main dining room and the front of the building had sustained the brunt of the damage. The other wing, where the pro shop was located, was more or less untouched, and it was from there that Rod emerged, helping to lead a handcuffed Rayanne toward the line of Pleasant Oaks police cruisers. Walt Briggs stood on the other side of Rayanne. Sage could see her mouth moving a mile a minute but could not hear her from where he sat. It didn't matter, he had a pretty good idea of what she was saying. She had spent months grooming Sage to take the fall and was now letting them know about what a madman he was.

It was an outrageous story, and he had his doubts that her ranting would convince anyone, even those half-wits on the Pleasant Oaks police force, but even if they did buy into her lies, he had little doubt he would be able to convince them she was the one behind all the murders and the country club bomb-ing, thanks to a trick he had learned from a dead man. While he was in the pro shop with Rayanne, he had been smart enough to turn on his phone's voice recorder. He was grateful that when the bomb knocked him across the parking lot, his phone hadn't sustained so much as a scratch. He made a mental note to leave a five-star review for the phone case he had purchased on Amazon.

Once Rayanne was safely loaded into the back of one of the Pleasant Oaks cruisers, Rod made his way over to where Sage was sitting.

"That looks pretty nasty," Rod said with a nod at Sage's bleeding forehead. "You want a lift to the hospital."

"I'm good," Sage said. "Look, I don't know what Rayanne told you back there, but—"

"Just more lies," Rod said.

"More lies?" Sage asked.

"Like that lie about you being too drunk to drive and leaving your car there," Rod said.

Sage had forgotten about that. He couldn't remember Rayanne driving him home, but neither could he remember driving himself home. His memory was foggy.

"When you took off before, I thought maybe you headed over there to get your car. So I went to Rayanne's, found your car there, and noticed one of her earrings on the driver's side mat. It just felt off to me."

"She could have moved it out of her driveway," Sage said.

"Well, she said you left it parked out front," Rod said. "And I never told you about this, but I don't know if you remember that day you had me come down to the coffee shop to talk to that friend of yours, Ambrose Radcliffe?" Sage nodded, and Rod continued. "Well, she hurried out of the building right before me. I wouldn't have thought anything of it, but she mentioned his name one day, claimed you had said it when you were being interviewed about driving off with that high school girl, but you didn't."

"She killed him," Sage said. "His body is inside."

"Jesus," Rod muttered. "All these years I worked with her, and I never had any idea."

"I have her recorded confession." Sage pulled out his phone, but before he brought it up, he noticed a text had come in from his father.

"What is it?" Rod asked.

"I think I'm going to take you up on that offer to drive me to the hospital," Sage said.

"Feeling a little woozy?" Rod asked.

"My dad just texted me," Sage said. "My mother woke up from her coma."

52

JUSTIN HAD TRIED to beg off staying for dinner, but Sage's mom wouldn't hear of it.

"I'm not going to let you work your butt off all day and then not give you dinner," she said. "What kind of person would I be if I sent my family home without dinner?"

"I'm not family," Justin said sheepishly.

"Nonsense!" she cried. "You're as much family as Sage and his dad."

Justin could have pointed out that Sage and his father weren't actually family at all, but having spent the day moving furniture and boxes with the two men, he knew they were undeniably a father and son no matter what some DNA test said. So maybe the fact that over the past few months he had celebrated holidays and special occasions with the Dorians did make him a sort of honorary member of their family.

Sage had been a big help in claiming back his old life and his old name, which was extra helpful now that he had decided to enroll in college. Maybe he was a little old for a college fresh-man, but when the news came out that his actions had saved hundreds of lives and he was hailed as a hero, a local college had awarded him a full scholarship. He decided it would be a shame to waste that opportunity.

Because they had already loaded all the furniture onto the moving truck, dinner was Chinese food that they ate while sitting on plastic tubs and cardboard boxes. Even though Sage and Zoey were sharing a plastic tote and Mr. and Mrs. Dorian were perched together on a sturdy cardboard box, Justin didn't feel like a fifth wheel. Everyone seemed to go out of their way to make sure he was included, and he really felt like he was part of a family.

"I can't believe you two are really moving," Sage said.

After waking up from her coma, Kelly Dorian had needed weeks and weeks of physical therapy, but her husband had been by her side the whole time. The two of them were separated before Rayanne threw a brick through Kelly's kitchen window and hit her in the head, but the terrible accident had brought her and her husband back together. So when she was finally getting around again on her own and Zoey had found a buyer for the house, the Dorians decided to buy a condo near the beach in Delaware.

"We won't be that far away," Kelly promised. "You better make sure fixing up that guest bedroom is a top priority. Because we'll be up to visit a lot."

About a month ago, Sage and Zoey bought a fixer-upper house and moved in together. They had even offered to fix up an apartment over the garage for Justin, but he decided to stay in a place of his own for now, a slightly less crappy apartment than his last one, and it had the advantage of being right near his college.

Getting his name and his old life back was a huge and positive change for Justin, but it wasn't the only big event. Immediately after he had called to warn the country club staff about the bomb, the voices stopped completely. It was as if once he had done his duty and saved all those people, the voices decided to release him. Though he appreciated the silence and was relieved to be free of the burden of clairaudience, he also felt a bit strange and disconnected. He wasn't used to being in the dark about everything. Uncertainty could be a bit frightening.

His own future was a mystery to him. That was normal, but it still worried him. He wasn't sure what he would do once he graduated college. Hell, he hadn't even figured out what he was going to major in. Sometimes he wished his old friends from the spirit realm would whisper something useful in his ear.

"Justin! Heads up!" Sage shouted.

Justin snapped to attention when he saw a fortune cookie sailing through the air toward him. He managed to catch it, but just barely. Around him, the rest of his adopted family was crinkling plastic and breaking open cookies.

"What's yours say?" Zoey asked him.

Justin broke open his cookie and slipped the little strip of paper out. As he read the words there, a smile spread across his face. Maybe he couldn't hear the voices in his head anymore, but perhaps they hadn't gone completely silent.

A lifetime of happiness lies ahead of you read the words printed on the fortune. And as he looked up at the smiling faces of his newfound family, he knew it was true.

GET A FREE BOOK!

Hi, this is Alissa. I hope you enjoyed reading *Haunted Houses* as much as I enjoyed writing it!

If you enjoy thrillers and would like to learn about new ones I have coming out, I'd love to keep in touch with my The Adventure Continues email newsletter, which I send out each month or so.

Sign up today and get a free ebook copy of my thriller novella *In the Bag*. To sign up and start reading your copy of *In the Bag* today, head over to alissagrosso.com.

A FAVOR TO ASK

I know you're busy, but it would mean a lot to me if you could take a few minutes out of your day to write a review of this book. Reviews help authors by improving search rankings and letting other readers know if this is a book they would enjoy reading.

I am eternally grateful to readers who take the time to leave reviews on the sites of the retailers where they've purchased my books.

ALSO BY ALISSA GROSSO

For Adults

Haunted Houses (Culver Creek No. 3)

Factory Girls (Culver Creek No. 2)

Up the Creek (Culver Creek No. 1)

In the Bag

Girl Most Likely to Succeed

For Young Adults

Unnamed Roads

Shallow Pond

Ferocity Summer

Popular

ABOUT THE AUTHOR

Alissa Grosso is the author of several books for adults and teens. When she's not busy writing she's probably hanging out with her boyfriend Ron or perhaps she's creating some new digital illustrations. Originally from New Jersey, she now resides in Bucks County, Pennsylvania.

For more information visit:

alissagrosso.com